Praise for Myla Goldberg's

the *f*alse friend

"Wondrous. . . . A constantly surprising story. . . . Goldberg draws readers into a world in which people don't have single, lifelong identities. They morph."
—*The Asheville Citizen-Times* (North Carolina)

"Captivating. . . . Pitch perfect. . . . An irresistible story of a woman trying to reconcile her ever-warping memories, memories that ultimately are proven to be the most 'False Friend' of all." —*Chattanooga Times Free Press* (Tennessee)

"Celia's journey causes us to examine the impact of our words and deeds, the reliability of our memories, and how these things shape the people we ultimately grow to be."
—*Bay City Times* (Michigan)

"The term *mean girls* is elevated to a new level in Goldberg's moody novel. . . . This is a layered, understated novel about the complex, ambiguous nature of memory and its effect on the dynamics of relationships. Great fodder for reading groups." —*Library Journal* (starred review)

Myla Goldberg

the *f*alse friend

Myla Goldberg is the author of several
books, including *Wickett's Remedy* and
the bestselling, critically acclaimed *Bee
Season*, which was widely translated and
adapted to film. She lives in Brooklyn,
New York.

www.mylagoldberg.com

ALSO BY MYLA GOLDBERG

the *f*alse friend

Anchor Books
A Division of Random House, Inc.
New York

the *f*alse
friend

A NOVEL

Myla
Goldberg

FIRST ANCHOR BOOKS EDITION, AUGUST 2011

Copyright © 2010 by Myla Goldberg

The Library of Congress has cataloged the Doubleday edition as follows:
Goldberg, Myla.
The false friend / by Myla Goldberg. — 1st ed.
p. cm.
I. Title.
PS3557.O35819F35 2010
813'.54—dc22   2010003844

Anchor ISBN: 978-0-307-39070-7

Book design by Maria Carella

www.anchorbooks.com

Printed in the United States of America
10 9 8 7 6 5 4 3 2 1

FOR MY DAUGHTERS

At this point I must explain that absolution by means of repentance is possible for all sins with the exception of three. One of these is leading people astray by establishing an evil practice or issuing a wrong decision, since the damage done cannot be repaired. Of one who commits such a sin Scripture says: Whoso causeth the upright to go astray in an evil way, he shall fall himself into his own pit.

—Saadia Gaon, *Kitab al-Amanat wal-l'tikadat*
(The Book of Belief and Opinions)

We cannot become the person we long to be by ignoring the persons we have been.

—Richard Hirsch, *Mahzor LeYamim Nora'im:*
Prayerbook for the Days of Awe

the *f*alse friend

CHAPTER *1*

The sight of a vintage VW bug dredged Djuna Pearson from memory. "Ladybug," Djuna said into Celia's ear as casually as ever, as if this were not the first time that voice had been heard in twenty-one years. Downtown Chicago streamed around Celia in a blur of wing tips and pumps. She stared, seasick, at the gleam of a discarded foil wrapper. When Celia shut her eyes, Djuna materialized behind her closed lids, the two of them sharing the backseat of Mrs. Pearson's Volvo, posting lookout for their favorite car. "Ladybug," Djuna called, and at the sound of that familiar, long-forgotten voice, a false wall crumbled to reveal a maze of other rooms, Djuna standing at the center of each one.

Djuna Pearson had appeared at the desk in front of Celia on the first day of fifth grade, the new girl's dark ponytail tied back with ribbon, stray hairs feathering a slender nape like enameled porcelain. Djuna had excellent posture, and for this Celia decided to hate her. By the second week of school they were friends of an intensity that summoned hangers-on. Their three most ardent satellites were Josie; Leanne; and Becky, the best friend Djuna had replaced. At any given moment Djuna and Celia were a party the others were desperate to attend, or a traffic accident too spectacular to avoid.

As the last pedestrians left the curb, the WALK sign counted three, two, one. Celia remained in place, replaying the culmination of a playground argument as if it were a home movie.

It had been windy and Celia was wearing her favorite hat, the one with the yellow pompon. With each gust the pompon shifted—a slight, ticklish feeling, as if a bird had chosen the top of Celia's head to make its nest. Djuna had stood facing Celia, the tips of their noses not six inches apart. It must have been Djuna's turn to be outraged because her face was so contorted that her chapped bottom lip had started to bleed. When she yelled, "Your hat is stupid!" Celia heard the words, felt the heat of Djuna's fury, but had been more interested in watching the fissure in the stretched, pink skin at the bottom curve of her best friend's mouth turn a darker shade of red. Celia remembered the pause, her utter calm before replying, "Your lips are ugly," as if it were a fact to be memorized for a test later on. Djuna spun away, her ponytail slicing an angry arc through the air. When she turned around to scream, "I hate you!" bodies stilled across the blacktop, recess paused to pay homage to a greater power.

Their reconciliations involved passed notes and the pretense that nothing had happened. During the lulls between storms, they spent hours playing in Djuna's room, pretending at belonging to a vast family of orphaned sisters drawn on successive pages of a spiral-bound notebook. Djuna designed the clothes, elaborate ensembles of petticoats and lace that resembled wedding cakes. Celia drew heads that were mostly hair and eyes. One of these afternoons returned to her, a sensory snapshot. She had been staying for dinner and could recall the scent of Mrs. Pearson's cooking wafting upstairs. Residual light from the fading day had cast Djuna's features in pale grays, making her seem like a statue of a girl brought temporarily to life. They sat on Djuna's bed contemplating a notebook page thick with sisters, the pair meant to represent them the most beautifully drawn of all. "We will never be closer to anyone than we are to each other right now," Djuna vowed, to which Celia had agreed with all the certainty eleven years of life could provide. Twenty-one years later, she realized it was still true.

When the WALK sign returned, Celia crossed with everyone else, then stopped at the opposite curb to stare at the corner she'd left behind. It was the same instinct that drove others to mark the scenes of accidents and crimes with homemade wooden crosses, with photos and candles. Memorials created the illusion of a sympathetic landscape. Celia looked for some fresh stain, or a crack in the pavement, but saw nothing to mark the demise of her previous self.

Spring had scrapped the need for a jacket, and a breeze snaked inside Celia's sleeve. In the heat of the afternoon, she and Djuna had fashioned their coats into capes in order to streak downhill from the bus, arms outthrust, their coat capes flapping behind them. When Celia didn't slouch, they were the same height but Djuna's arms were longer. Djuna had double-jointed fingers and could waggle each fingertip at its top knuckle. At the bottom of the hill they would throw themselves onto the nearest lawn. Djuna insisted that she could hear the grass grow when she pressed her ear to the ground.

It was not yet nine A.M. and Celia wanted to close her eyes and be draped over a shoulder to be carried home like a sleep-clobbered child. Instead she used her reflection in a storefront window to examine a softer, more impressionable landscape. Her nose and chin had sharpened, and her hair was darker than it once had been. She had lost the baby fat that had once made her cheeks pinchable, but her eyes were the same pale blue. Djuna could have dowsed from those features a smaller face now outgrown. Celia searched the opposite corner one last time, hoping to conjure Djuna from that single remembered word, but the voice she had heard was light from an extinguished star.

Above the doors of Celia's destination, STATE OF ILLINOIS BUILDING was carved in stone, those words a former title belt worn in reverse reflection by the mirrored facade of the new champion across the street. The Thompson Center contained an El station, a shopping mall, and most of the state agencies that had once endowed its older neighbor. Celia's building was called the Bilandic now, demoted to glorifying a former mayor, the Illinois Auditor General's office the most distinguished among the agencies it had retained. Celia had always preferred her building, but had the Auditor General's office moved with the rest, she would not have been on the street that morning. Like the personnel of the Lottery Department and the Elections Board, she would have traveled from the El station to her office door without ever having to step outside. She would not have seen the red car. For the rest of her life she might have enjoyed the illusion that she was no more monstrous than anybody else.

I think, therefore I am is too vague. We are, because we remember. As each new present blinks out, its heart is weighed and then judged, preserved in mental amber or consumed. Before, Celia's memory had functioned present but hidden, as necessary and neglected as a pancreas or a spleen. Now it had revealed itself to be a twenty-one-year cheat.

Celia crossed the lobby, rode the elevator, and arrived at her office the way it is possible to drive for miles hypnotized by the highway, then found herself standing at the receptionist's desk with Helene, Gary, Gloria, and Steven all staring at her.

"Celia?" Helene asked. Celia felt a hand on her arm. "Are you okay?"

Celia turned toward the voice as five fugitive words came out of hiding. "My best friend is dead," she said.

CHAPTER 2

By the next day, Celia was on an eastbound plane. Her window seat represented the culmination of Helene's instruction to go home, to take compassionate leave for the funeral it had been assumed she would need to attend. Every intervening moment—the previous morning's backward commute on the outbound El; the moment Celia told Huck about Djuna; the awkward phone call to her parents; the last-minute purchase of her plane ticket home—all these had felt unsurvivable until she had survived them. The dogs had helped. During the dim, empty hours leading up to the time of Huck's return, Celia had lain less asleep than in a state of suspended animation, succored by the sound of Bella's steady breathing and

Sylvie's warmth beside her on the bed. The dogs had met Huck at the front door, then lain at Celia's feet as she told Huck what she remembered, speaking into the crook of his arm as if to protect her words from exposure to light.

All five of them—Celia, Djuna, Becky, Josie, and Leanne—were supposed to have gone home on their respective buses, but walking had been that day's buried fulcrum, the shared secret around which the rest of the day had turned. Jensenville Elementary lay along a wooded, curving two-lane road with no sidewalks, its sole pedestrian the occasional doomed possum. Rumors of the woods abounded. The forest was said to conceal an abandoned stable with a haunted horse skeleton; a derelict quarry filled with glowing water; a moldy mansion from inside which a warlock lured children with promises of candy and then beat them with his belt. They had refuted these stories and then repeated them word for word. They were frightened of the woods and in love with being frightened. To walk along Ripley Road was an unthinkable transgression that could not be denied once it had been conceived.

Celia and Djuna had been fighting, their anger so sharp that after twenty-one years the memory still made Celia flinch. The force of their argument had propelled them past the others and around a curve, nothing but road and trees stretching in either direction. The gravel shoulder along the road's edge was just wide enough to walk two abreast, but Djuna pulled ahead of Celia and veered into the woods. They had fought so often, over the littlest things, that the cause of that day's fury had merged in Celia's mind with the sound of fracturing under-brush as she threaded her way between trees in an attempt to follow. So much could have happened differently. If Celia had taken the same path as Djuna, she might have seen what was coming. Had Djuna entered the woods at a different point, she might have avoided the danger. Had they not been fighting to begin with, they might not have left the road. In any of those instances, the afternoon would have been indistinguishable from countless others.

Instead, Celia watched Djuna fall. One minute she was there, and the next the earth had swallowed her up.

Celia may have called into the silence. She may have stood there, waiting for Djuna to rise from the undergrowth. Maybe she meant to teach Djuna a lesson. Perhaps she thought her most secret, shameful wish had just come true. The unadult mind is immune to logic or foresight, unschooled by conse-quence, and endowed with a biblical sense of justice. The only thing more appalling to Celia than these excuses was the child's act they contrived to explain. When Djuna failed to reappear or make a sound of any kind, Celia had not tried to help. Instead she'd retraced her own path through the trees to return to the road, then back around the curve to where Josie, Becky, and Leanne were still waiting. She told them that Djuna had gotten into a stranger's car, and they had nodded like a trio of marionettes, the first in a town of fifty thousand to believe her.

Celia had envisioned a spectrum of doomsday scenarios to accompany her confession. None were remotely fulfilled. Huck certainly didn't leave her. Instead, at the moment she had been dreading, he became very still. "Oh dear," he had said like a nineteenth-century schoolgirl, surprise making him demure.

It had taken only a few seconds for the Huck she knew to return—sensible, fast-thinking Huck who specialized in contingencies—but the immediate effect of Celia's words was to render him rudderless, a sight almost as frightening as anything she had forecast. Not until she was lying insomniac in Huck's arms did she realize why she had gotten him so wrong. The eleven-year-old girl she had described to Huck was a stranger. Only Celia recognized that girl and what she had done. Neither the sound of Bella nor the cradle of Huck's exuded warmth had trumped the loneliness of that knowledge, a secret she did not wish to keep.

On Celia's annual Christmas trips home with Huck, the packed holiday plane felt like a multifamily station wagon, the stewardess dispensing extra packets of snack mix to stave off are-we-there-yets. Today's flight was half empty, and rather than bartering with Huck for the window, Celia had a row of seats to herself. The first time she had ever flown back east had been with him, her solo drive condensed to a trip the length of a Hollywood movie. She'd been reluctant to give up seven hundred miles of highway, her progress measured in tanks of gas and cans of Dr Pepper, her thoughts ordered incrementally with each dashed yellow line. That yearly road trip had been a natural extension of her local driving expeditions, weekend explorations of her adopted state that had become as much a habit as the Sunday paper. Celia savored charting a course on a map to steer by, a simple objective stated and then achieved. Framed by a windshield, details of landscape caught her eye that she otherwise might have missed: a hand-painted billboard, a dry-stacked stone wall. Sometimes the sound of her tires against different surfaces—smooth bitumen, weathered asphalt, the metal grid of a bridge—had even suggested new poems.

She and Huck had met when he introduced himself after a senior reading. He'd praised a sonnet whose beginning had come to her while she'd been driving over a covered bridge in Long Grove that seemed to say, *No songs, no songs, no songs.* The reading had been held at the Reynolds student center, where Celia's ubiquity often got her mistaken for an employee. That semester, she'd been treasurer for two student advocacy groups, co-editor of the campus literary journal, and Urgent Action Coordinator for the campus chapter of Amnesty International. Huck had been a stranger to Reynolds. A hazel-eyed, strong-jawed creature without her cluttered schedule, he'd sparked in Celia the same detached, appreciative desire she felt for the grace of an animal observed in the wild—until she discovered that he had not learned to drive until his sophomore year of college. This exotic, absurd fact made him seem attainable. Instead of acquiescing to Huck's interest, she began courting him with her car, wooing him with careful itineraries: old routes west of the lake that passed woods and prairies; a pilgrimage to Calumet's smiley-faced water towers. Her solitary car trips came to an end, the obscure poetic utterances of the road replaced by boundless miles of two-way conversation, though even after she had won Huck he remained impervious to the more subtle charms of a twelve-hour drive. To quell her nervousness on their first flight—their relationship had never traveled so far or so fast—she had packed their traditional roadside picnic, complete with red-checkered napkins for their seat-back trays, their plates of cold chicken sparking longing and envy across the aisle.

This morning Celia had given no thought to even basic airplane comforts—a water bottle, a mindless magazine—but when she reached into her carry-on, there was the familiar red-checked napkin, wrapped around a bagel. Huck would be at school by now, charming a room of teenagers into caring about the Louisiana Purchase or the Great Migration, but in that moment she felt him inviting her to enjoy the pleasure of a picnic at thirty thousand feet, and the sight of cirrus clouds outside her oval window.

When the plane's descent through the clouds revealed a green patchwork instead of quilted whites and grays, Celia wondered if she had somehow boarded the wrong flight. After years of December arrivals, she had forgotten the place contained more than one season.

The breeze off the tarmac as she crossed to the gate brought thoughts of Bella and Sylvie alone in the apartment, enslaved to the approaching jingle of the dog walker's keys. The girls had been with Celia so long that their preferred walking times in late morning and mid-afternoon turned Celia restless wherever she happened to be. She had visited the dog shelter directly after college graduation, thinking about volunteering. Instead, she'd adopted two scrawny shepherd/Lab mix puppies that had been found tied to a MERGE sign on a traffic median, and had gratefully devoted herself to their rehabilitation. Huck had been in Baltimore, teaching at a summer program for precocious teens, and though they had met only recently, his months away had felt too long. Whether Celia adopted Bella and Sylvie to fill the unexpected void or to test Huck's resolve on his return was rendered moot by the speed of his infatuation. Huck joked that Bella and Sylvie wouldn't forgive them if they ever broke up, but it was true. From the start, the four of them had belonged to one another. In restaurants when Celia wasn't too hungry, she ordered whatever she thought would be most eagerly gobbled from its take-home container. She couldn't fly into Syracuse International without imagining Bella gleefully barking at arriving and departing planes, poor Sylvie cowering on one of the grassy stripes between runways, awaiting rescue.

Each Christmas she and Huck rented a car at the terminal, but over the phone her mother had insisted on meeting her at the airport. The phone call had been a disaster. Celia had fooled herself into thinking it would be possible to announce her arrival the next day without having to explain it, a delusion that had not lasted much beyond hello. "Has she been found?" Noreen asked after Celia mentioned Djuna, the first time anyone in her family had spoken that name in over twenty years. Celia was stymied by anything but the most simple answer to her mother's question. She needed to wait until she could gauge the effect of her words on her mother's face.

They had not needed to discuss where to meet. It was not a big airport, the second of its two terminals an artifact from a more prosperous age. At the base of the Terminal A escalator, among those disguising their waiting by talking on cell phones, or feigning absorption in magazines, Noreen Durst stood stone-still, her eyes fixed on her daughter. The sight of her mother waiting to claim her on a weekday afternoon made Celia feel like a child sent home from school.

"Sweetheart," Noreen said. She looked up to meet her daughter's face. Celia bent down as she had ever since fourteen had turned her tall, but today felt different. Noreen had replaced her regular shampoo with something more cosmetic that garbled her scent. Celia felt like she was kissing a stranger.

"Where's Dad?" Celia asked. He would be parked in the loading zone beyond the sliding glass doors, but the pretense of a search allowed Celia to trade her mother's perfumed hair for the neutral air of baggage claim.

"In the car, but I didn't want to miss a minute. Oh, Celie," Noreen said, "it's so nice that you've come." Her hand reached toward her daughter's face and then stopped. "You look fine," she confirmed. "A little pale, maybe."

Celia wanted to apologize for everything: for the oblique phone call, for their presence in the airport, for the schedule her arrival had interrupted. "I didn't sleep well," she said. She gazed across the top of her mother's head and saw her mother's scalp, luminous beneath a carefully constructed helmet of thinning hair the same dark brown as her own.

"Your eyes are a bit raccoony," Noreen said. "But we'll fix that. I made up two beds because I wasn't sure. There's the one in the guest room . . . but I, for one, can't stand sleeping in a big bed when I'm all alone in it, so I also set up the one in your old bedroom, just in case."

They had reached the luggage carousel. Dark-hued roller bags circled at glacial speed. People leaned forward to look, then back, a synchronized ripple of motion.

"The guest room will be fine," Celia said. A tent in the backyard would have been fine, a space on the floor of the garage. Her mother's presence amplified the shame that had found Celia in Chicago, seemed to extend it beyond the length of her body. A pine-green bag appeared at the top of the luggage portal. Celia leaned forward.

"I thought so." Noreen sighed. "You've always been so much more independent. I don't think your father and I have ever slept apart for more than—"

Celia patted her mother's arm. "Mom, it's okay," she said. "Huck wanted to be here. I was the one who told him to wait. It's almost the end of the quarter. Coming today would have meant sticking his kids with a sub, and his sixth-period class has the AP test in less than a month."

"Of course," Noreen affirmed, and began crying. "I'm sorry," she said. She dabbed at her face with a crumpled tissue. "I'm a little . . . I didn't sleep too well last night either. I was just so excited." Her smile was lopsided, her lips unequal to the task of its formation.

Warren was parked at the curb directly beyond the exit doors in a new gray sedan, a Bud Powell tune streaming from its open windows. At the sight of his daughter, he leaned across to open the front passenger-side door.

"Welcome home, kiddo!" he called. His voice was barely audible above the torrent of piano, but his expression was as unambiguous as a wagging tail. Celia knew no other human creature who greeted all he loved with such uncomplicated joy.

"Warren, turn that down!" Noreen scolded, smiling all the while. She turned to Celia. "He got us here forty minutes early, just in case."

Celia slid back the front passenger seat to accommodate her legs, then realized that for the first time since she was fourteen, driver and passenger seats were unaligned. Her father had begun to shrink. Celia quickly slid her seat a notch closer in.

"What do you think?" Warren asked, gesturing at the car's interior. He was wearing the same leather driving gloves as always and the most recent driving cap Celia had given him for Father's Day.

"It's what you always get!" Celia moaned. "When you said silver, I was picturing something sporty."

"It is sporty!" he said, pointing. "Look, a moonroof!"

"It's a Camry, Dad."

"Of course it's a Camry." Warren shrugged. "The Camry is an excellent car."

"Then why trade it in every other year?"

Warren winked. "Because, my sweet, I am trying to impress a certain lady."

From the backseat, Celia's mother giggled.

Hand clasping the steering wheel like a favorite dance partner, Warren was assured without being aggressive, could converse without missing a turn. He once described his weekly six-hour commute to court Noreen—Celia's mother was in college while he was posted to Fort Letterkenny—as one of the

happiest times in his life. Celia understood precisely how that
could be true.

"So how are things in Chi-town?" he asked, as if they
shared the front seat every Tuesday afternoon. "You finished
with the hospitals?"

"Back in January," Celia said. "Now it's beverage vending."

Celia hadn't known what a performance auditor was until
halfway through graduate school, when her advisor had suggested that her reluctance to commit to any one aspect of public policy might make her an ideal candidate. She'd joined the
Auditor General's performance division the month she gradu-
ated, and was assigned to a team examining the Illinois Racing
Board. For the next nine months Celia had surrendered herself to horseracing. She visited racetracks and talked with on-
site veterinarians, becoming versed in the medical lexicon of
butes and milk shakes and Lasix. She was permitted into deten-
tion barns as winning horses were bathed and cooled out. She
never got used to the drug testing, flinching at the blood draws
even when the doctor was quick with the needle and the
horses unperturbed. By the following spring the audit was
complete—the research done, the field interviews conducted,
the report written and filed—and she was studying foster family placements through child protective services.

Each investigation was an intellectual road trip to a place
of previously locked doors, a chance to peer at a new, obscure
corner of civic life through a magnifying lens. It felt to Celia a
bit like assembling a sand painting grain by grain and then
destroying it once the pattern was complete, but the job satisfied her appetite for variety, optimized her long-standing indus-

triousness. In high school and college, she had signed petitions and organized rallies on faith, unsure she was making a difference, but within a year of her first auditing assignments, the State Assembly had responded to her division's recommendations, drafting legislation that better aligned state animal drug-testing standards with national practices, and providing funds to improve foster family recruitment and training techniques. It mystified Celia that more people didn't want to do what she did, and that still fewer were interested in hearing about it—but even that came to feel like an asset. The very words *Performance Auditor* were an excellent cocktail-party litmus test to divine the curious from the incurious, the affable from the petty. Those who didn't greet her job title with a polite smile and a quick glance over the rest of the room were rewarded with stories of drug surveillance via helicopter during a study of the Police Criminal Investigations Division, or an impromptu embalming-room anatomy lesson during an examination of the Funeral Directors' Licensing Board. Huck loved these stories, repeating them whenever he got the chance, but Warren's interest went beyond anecdote. When Celia described to her father Chicago's tobacco tax distributions, or the varying failure rates from the city's emissions tests, she felt like she was offering game stats to a rabid baseball fan, a transaction Noreen observed with the detached enjoyment of a zoo visitor at feeding time.

"Jeremy says hello," Celia's mother said once the air had cleared. "He and Pam would like to drive down to visit while you're here."

"Your brother got promoted," Warren added. "They made

him a senior adjuster, which is good because they're going to need the extra money now that Number Two is on the way."

"Pam is pregnant again?"

Celia's sister-in-law had been pregnant recently enough that Celia could picture Pam's face hovering palely above a blue maternity dress, her Christmas dinner napkin lying on her rounded belly like a picnic blanket stranded on an alp.

"Three months as of last week." From the tone of her mother's voice Celia could tell she was smiling. "They had wanted two, just maybe not this close together."

"It's what you'd call a happy accident," Warren pronounced, nodding in agreement with himself.

When they arrived at their traditional roadside diner, Celia was unsurprised to find the interior unchanged down to their usual corner booth, though the place was called Jonnie's now instead of the Treeview and nothing tasted as good—the onion rings no longer homemade, the soup saltier than before.

"When was the last time you saw spring in New York State?" her father asked from behind his hamburger.

"It's been a while," she said. The influence of her father's conviviality was wearing off like a painkiller that stops masking a dull ache. Celia remembered the reason she had come.

"You ought to visit again in September, when the leaves are going crazy," her father said. "And bring that boyfriend of yours. The poor guy has only ever seen the Southern Tier when it's frozen over."

"Warren—"

Warren waved the voice away. "I bet if Huck got a taste of what it can be like here in the fall—"

"Warren—"

"It's okay, Nor."

Warren rested his arm along the top of the booth where a taller woman's shoulders would have been, his shirt sleeve adorning the back of Noreen's head like a clever hat. In each other's presence, Celia's parents became a single organism, a consolidation that had occurred too long ago for Celia to ever undo. From across the table, Celia saw two versions of the same smile.

"We're awfully glad you've come, Cee Cee," Warren said. "When you start getting older, you begin to appreciate what's truly important, and you visiting like this . . . well, it means a lot to us."

Celia was briefly tempted to confirm her visit as a gift they could congratulate themselves for being given. Instead, she turned toward the window. In winter, the scenery was beautiful in a stark way, the bare skeletons of trees black against the frozen hills. Now it was all green.

"Is there anything special you'd like to do while you're here?" Noreen coaxed, as if trying to persuade Celia to eat her green beans. "There's a new restaurant in Oswego we could try, and if the weather's good I was thinking it might be fun to hike around the lake."

"Sure, Mom." Celia tried to keep her voice even. "Look, I'm sorry I was so abrupt on the phone yesterday, but now that I'm here—"

"Oh no, dear," Noreen interrupted. "We understand perfectly. Phones are terrible for personal conversations. Phones . . ." She gestured at the tables around them. ". . . restaurants. Some things are much better left to discuss in person, and in private. It's so important to be comfortable."

Celia's parents nodded in spontaneous unison, a pair of bobblehead dolls. Celia's mouth opened and shut. She had spent the plane ride preparing for this moment. Forcing the words back down felt like dry-swallowing pills. "But you asked what I'd like to do," she stammered, "and, well, I'm hoping to track down Leanne, Becky, and Josie. Not to mention Mrs. Pearson." She put her hands in her lap when she realized they were shaking.

Celia's mother blinked. "You mean Grace Pearson?"

"Who's Grace Pearson?" Warren asked.

"Grace Pearson is Grace Pearson," Noreen answered. "Dennis's wife."

"You mean the mother of Cee Cee's little friend—"

"Djuna," Celia said.

They all looked out the window at once. Spring foliage hedged the parking lot, obscuring the view. There was probably a store or a fenced-in yard just a few feet away, but from the diner it looked like the trees went on forever.

"Why do you want to see Grace Pearson?" Noreen asked in her guidance counselor voice, as if Grace Pearson were a college Celia shouldn't pin her hopes on.

"To talk to her," Celia said. "Her, and everyone else who was part of what happened back then."

Noreen dabbed at an imaginary spot on the table.

"Your mother's right," Warren said. "We'll get back home, you'll get a little rest, and then when you feel good and ready—"

"But do you know if she even still lives around here?" Celia asked.

Celia's father scrutinized his plate.

"Dennis left," Noreen said quietly, "but Grace stayed. I don't think she wanted . . . She didn't like the idea of going too far."

Eventually, the three of them returned to the car. For the rest of the trip, Noreen remained intent on the passing scenery, her elbow propped on her armrest, her chin cupped in her hands. Celia's identical pose in the front seat betrayed her as Noreen's daughter. Had she not so resembled her father, the driver whose jittery fingers picked at the custom-wrapped steering wheel might have been taken for someone hired to ferry his passengers to a place neither wanted to go.

CHAPTER 3

When Jensens were still made in Jensenville and America's rubber boot capital seemed as firmly rooted as a sycamore, the town built a stone arch carved on both sides with the words LET IT RAIN. After the factories had moved south and trains started skipping the local station, the arch remained, spanning the road like a tombstone. Depending on the direction being traveled, the inscription served as augury or epitaph. Leaving for college, Celia screamed those words loud enough to wind herself, and almost crashed into a stalled Ford Pinto. Each homecoming forced a new surrender.

Djuna appeared at the edge of Celia's vision as soon as Warren's car cleared the arch's shadow. As if to compensate for twenty-one years of banishment, there she was dancing by the corner drugstore waiting for the light to change; and there, in front of the post office where she had once fallen off her bike. Celia spotted Djuna striking poses before the defunct hobby shop, and a block later lounging on the bench beside the former stationery store. Trudy's Card and Gift had been turned into a combination head shop and skateboard outlet called Skate and Bake. Seasonal window displays of hearts, Easter eggs, shamrocks, and turkeys had been replaced by a handwritten sign—SMOKEING EQUIPMENT MEANT FOR TOBACCO ONLY—that spelled its own imminent demise. Celia was reminded of another window, papered with sun-faded albums and a sign that read VISIONS IN VINYL. The place had stunk of cat piss and mildew. Even breathing through her mouth, Celia had barely tolerated standing inside the store while Djuna flitted down its aisles, trying to flirt with men intent on rummaging through the used-record bins. That shop front had long ago been painted pink and rechristened ELECTROLYSIS BY ELYCE.

Djuna had disappeared by the time Celia reached the boarded-up dry cleaners at Elm and Main, its hazmat signs unchanged since the Reagan era. The prevailing high school wisdom had kids in search of a cheap buzz invading its basement to inhale fumes thrown off by moldering vats of solvent. Had Celia been around to witness her brother's high school years, she might have known if it was true. Beyond the dry cleaners, the streets bore the stamp of Jensenville's founding German émigrés. The best proof of their successful assimilation was the local pronunciation of "Beth-o-ven" and "Go-ee-thee" streets. Such phonetic butchery had been sidestepped by Schubert, an asset Warren and Noreen had considered along with their home's southern exposure and restored front porch before signing on the dotted line. Built before the cookie-cutter era of planned communities, the neighborhood's diverse arrangements of porches, pitched roofs, and dormer windows had been realized by an early twentieth-century abundance of materials and labor. Celia grew up taking such charms for granted, along with the bounty of school-aged children. Those not in public school had attended the Immaculate Heart of Mary, whose adjoining church had tolled the hours from nine to six, as well as the daily masses. Celia had learned to count by tallying the call to worship to its thirty-ninth ring, but the number remained a mystery until Randy Blocker, a Heart of Mary boy two doors down, had described the special fervency of Immaculate Heart's pastor for the number of lashes Christ received, extinguishing Celia's envy of plaid uniforms.

Since Celia's Midwestern migration, the pastor had retired and the church bells had fallen into disrepair, their stillness ringing in an age of stagnation. As children left for college, sluggish property values delayed the move that commonly cushioned the transition to retirement, creating a neighborhood of empty nests and muted seasons. The jingle of ice cream trucks stopped marking the arrival of spring. The lifeguard's whistle took on purely ceremonial functions as adult and all-swim merged. Successive Halloweens passed with fewer and fewer trick-or-treaters, until Warren and Noreen no longer even bothered with a token bowl of candy. On weekends, or for brief stretches during school holidays and summer vacations, grandchildren sporadically revived small patches of neighborhood lawn and sidewalk with bikes and roller skates, but then returned to whichever more abundant town their parents had chosen, leaving a neighborhood of nostalgic Nanas and PawPaws behind.

With the advent of Medicare and Social Security benefits, FOR SALE signs began appearing on front lawns. Aging hips and knees cashed out and traded stairs for single-floor plans in senior communities, or apartments in elevator buildings. In other places such migrations spurred rebirth, but even Jensenville University's new hires preferred to commute from towns less terminally postindustrial. Family homes were acquired by management companies for student rental, the real estate equivalent of inviting tent caterpillars into trees. Furniture appeared in front yards, and lawns became overgrown. Paint jobs peeled and faded. Three Christmases ago, Celia had returned home to the burnt shell of Randy Blocker's place, the result of a post-party tryst between a couch and a tenant's lit blunt. As recently as last December, its blackened carcass had remained half standing, scabbed over with ivy and graffiti. Only now, as Warren turned onto their block, did Celia notice a FOR SALE sign finally posted in the middle of the razed lot where, if she remembered correctly, the Blockers' downstairs bathroom had once been.

"The neighborhood's looking up," she almost joked and then didn't, thinking of the white-noise machine her mother had received last Christmas under the pretense of masking her father's nonexistent snores at two A.M., and not the hoots of drunken students. Celia and Jeremy took turns urging their parents to sell, but Warren was too house-proud to admit that his home improvements had been outpaced by the neighborhood's decline. When blasting stereos had nullified the pleasures of outdoor relaxation, he'd had the patio converted into an attached sunroom. Next came a seven-foot-tall privacy fence to shield the new sunroom from the sight of the barbecue pit that had replaced Mrs. Henley's flower garden. Celia had come to accept that only her father's death would spur change: her mother wouldn't want to live in the house without him, and he would never agree to live anywhere else.

"Are you tired, Celie?" Noreen asked the moment they had pulled into the driveway. "I was thinking we could go to the Chinese steakhouse for dinner."

"Cee Cee doesn't want to go there," Warren said. "It's overpriced and the staff isn't even Chinese. She's a Chicago girl! That sort of thing doesn't impress her."

"I could always cook," her mother offered. "I thought it might be nice to celebrate Celie's arrival, but we could just as easily do that tomorrow or the next day, once she's had some time to rest."

"I'm not tired," Celia said. Not since college had she visited home for more than a three-day weekend, and never without Huck.

"Well then, let's go out," Noreen reasoned. "We could go to Maximo's. Maxi always gets a kick out of seeing Celie, and they've still got that great fruit de mer appetizer with the octopus and the squid."

"Nor, why do you always insist on taking our daughter somewhere she got fired from as a waitress when she was seventeen?"

"She didn't get fired! Maxi just realized that she'd be better in the office—"

"Maximo's would be fine, Mom."

Celia opened her door and walked to the back of the car, hoping her father would pop the trunk, but instead he got out and used the key. She tried to beat him to the suitcase, then pretended not to hear his groan as he lifted it.

"Warren, you really should let Celie do that," her mother clucked. "Remember your back."

Warren shook his head. "Cee Cee took the effort to come all the way here. The least I can do is help her with her luggage." The two women hung back while he wrangled the bag onto the sidewalk and wheeled it to the front door.

Celia followed her mother up the drive, then looked across the street. The house opposite had once been a famously easy mark for Girl Scout cookies and Multiple Sclerosis Read-a-Thon sponsorships, but knocking had meant facing Mrs. Finch, who was childless and had a short leg. One year, hell-bent for a cookie merit badge, Celia had broken with tradition and accepted Mrs. Finch's invitation to come in. Seated on a musty brown couch beside a glass of powdered lemonade, she'd been introduced to the extensive doll family filling the greater portion of the living room, and was prompted to greet each doll by name. Celia's daring earned her an order for five boxes of Tagalongs, five Samoas, and five Thin Mints but made it impossible to deliver the goods, which she convinced her brother to leave on the doorstep. The living room window now contained an illuminated COORS sign. A gutted easy chair cultivated a dead spot on the front lawn.

Warren and Noreen were already inside by the time Celia reached the front walk, where she was ambushed by a memory of Djuna standing beside her. "Tell me where you hide your key," Djuna whispered, "and I'll be able to come anytime." Celia looked to the fake rock still beside the doormat, its putative cleverness undermined by the lack of decoy rocks or even a concealing hedge. She picked it up, flipped it over, and slid open the tab.

"Welcome home, darling," Noreen said, opening the door. Celia saw her mother's outstretched arm, her father standing sentinel beside the stairs. For a moment, it seemed as if the whole town was holding its breath, waiting for her to go in.

Warren's interest in home improvement aside, the house had changed very little since Celia's childhood. Inside the front entryway was the small enamel painting of a verdant field that inspired thoughts of creamed spinach. Looking at it now, Celia could practically feel her spirit shrivel to the creature she'd been at sixteen. It did not help that the family photo gallery leading to the kitchen was glaringly out-of-date. The newest picture was from Jeremy's community college graduation nine years back: he was gaunt but clean-shaven, his smile equal parts pride and relief. This was preceded by an enlarged snapshot of Celia receiving her undergraduate degree. In the most recent family portrait, Jeremy was growing out his hair but had yet to pierce his ears, and Celia was wearing a Cornell T-shirt. The picture dated from Celia's final high school year, a few months shy of her decision to flee west and several grade levels before her brother began snorting dope in his bedroom.

For years there'd been talk of a photo that would include Jeremy's burgeoning family as well as Huck, but so far the only sign of the Dursts' survival into the twenty-first century was a framed picture of Daniel. The grandson's photo overshadowed his parents' wedding portrait in the living room, which eclipsed a framed poem on display since Celia had won a statewide writing contest in high school. All three objects languished on a forlorn coffee table whose charms were annulled by the discomfort of the adjacent heirloom couch. The rest of that least-lived-in room, devoted to Warren's jazz habit, had sparked one of Celia and Djuna's epic fights. After jointly vandalizing one of Mr. Pearson's American Mathematical Society journals, Djuna had wanted to raid Warren's record collection, but Celia had refused. Thanks in part to her vigilance, everything in that portion of the room had remained intact: the custom record cabinets, the audiophile turntable Celia had been born knowing not to touch, the ancient leather chair in which her father sat wearing oversized headphones, playing his recordings at volumes no one else could bear, insisting LPs delivered greater fidelity than anything invented since.

From the kitchen, Celia heard the clink of stemware, followed by the *shump* of the refrigerator being opened. When she was small, her mother's wine had been kept in the door, a topple-prone arrangement that resulted in sporadic compositions of Chablis and shattered glass. At about the same time that juice boxes began appearing in Celia's lunches, a cardboard carton with a plastic tap became a permanent fixture on the fridge's right-hand side. Djuna had been the one to observe that sneaking a sip was an undetectable crime. Noreen's custom was a single glass at dinner, occasionally prefaced by a late afternoon tasting. This sole parental vice attested to a temperate streak Celia thought she had inherited. She had always assumed her brother was made of different stuff. She'd been halfway through college when Jeremy's grades began to slip. During her brief visits home, when she'd caught glimpses of a silent, glaring teenager with headphones grafted onto his ears, she'd admired her brother's precocity. Not until she'd been contemplating colleges, toward the end of her own high school career, had it occurred to her to rebel. Jeremy's ongoing transformation had constituted a regular segment of her parents' upbeat, long-distance telephone calls. Their cheerful insistence on his normalcy had persisted until the phone rang early one morning during Celia's junior year. Even when they told her Jeremy was in a coma, it was not until Celia heard the word *overdose* that she realized drugs had been involved all along. Now she wondered if Jeremy's addiction was a variant of what had possessed her just that once with Djuna in the woods. Their impulses had differed mainly in trajectory. Celia had aimed outward. Her brother had not.

Warren was halfway up with his daughter's suitcase, muffled grunts marking his slow progress. Celia dawdled with her coat, waiting until the sounds ceased before joining him upstairs. She had learned about his osteoarthritis last Christmas with her mother's gift of a bathing suit for lap therapy at the college pool. During her brief visits home, Celia watched for unfamiliar pills at breakfast and scanned medicine cabinets for recent prescriptions in order to restock her own mental formulary of questions. Only once, when Noreen found a lump in her breast, had Celia's parents ever volunteered medical info. Their preferred method was to wait until asked or until the danger had passed, calling Celia after a trip to the hospital for a cold that had turned into pneumonia, or after chest pains proved to be indigestion—proud each time of having spared her, impervious to the upset their deferments provoked.

"How's the knee?" Celia asked.

Warren shrugged without turning around, making a show of wheeling the suitcase behind him. "It's different on different days. It's always worse in cold weather."

"It's not cold today," Celia said.

"It's not so bad today," he replied. When they reached the guest room he leaned over as if to lift the bag onto the bed, then stopped and left it where it was.

The bedroom was the smallest of the four. No one remembered how it came to be called the Scottish Suite, only that the tartan wallpaper had preceded their tenancy, the nickname permitting them to treat the room as a sign of family irony and not aesthetic laziness. Noreen had midwifed a bevy of Halloween costumes on the everlasting Singer that now languished in one corner gathering dust. In high school, the room's wallpaper had come to symbolize all that was intolerable to Celia about living at home: her father's tuneless humming; her mother's copious bowls of snack foods; her parents' joint enthusiasm for whatever moronic interest gripped her brother. At the first sign of guests, she would flee upstairs to make sure the door was shut, one of several small ways she'd attempted to survive her teenage mortification at being someone's daughter. The first time Celia brought Huck home, she ran halfway up the stairs before turning back around. Pulling Huck aside, she'd described their sleeping arrangements in a grave whisper, as if the Scottish Suite might send him flying back to Chicago.

Once upon a time, this sort of thing had constituted a confession.

"You know, your mother set up your old bed down the hall," her father offered as they gazed at the room's foldout couch. "The one in here isn't exactly the most comfortable thing in the world."

The mattress in the Scottish Suite sagged like a swayback horse and creaked at the thought of movement. After Huck's inaugural visit, Celia had requested a better bed but Noreen had refused: they would upgrade in the event of wedding guests. Celia and Huck had adapted by ravishing one another on the floor beside the sewing table. Though Celia's mother had long ago knit Huck his own Christmas stocking, the foldout atrocity endured, the last outward symbol of Noreen's abiding hope for her daughter.

"Huck will be here this weekend," Celia said. "It seems silly to switch back and forth."

"Huck's a good man," her father said, his fingers tapping at her bag's pull-out handle. "I suppose you talk to him about things . . . when things happen?"

"I tell Huck everything." Celia's internal clock was confounded by the thought that at this time yesterday she had been in her bedroom in Chicago, waiting for Huck to come home.

"That's good." Warren nodded, backing away. "That's always been what your mother and I have done."

Celia's father retreated to the hallway. From the neighboring bedroom she heard the creaking bedsprings that announced his daily catnap. More than at any other time, her father looked his age when asleep. Years after the advent of gray hairs and thickening waistlines, Celia continued to be shocked by the progress of her parents' aging. In dizzying moments of delayed recognition, mental snapshots in her mind's billfold were rendered obsolete. She would notice the loosening skin along her father's jaw, the dark pouches beneath his eyes that sleep no longer erased. As her mother buttoned her coat, blue-gray veins would stand out from the collapsing skin of her hands, a trait exclusive to Celia's sole memory of her grand-mother, a seemingly ancient woman who had died at sixty-eight, an age that no longer seemed terribly old.

Celia returned downstairs to the den, where Noreen filled the leftmost of the matching recliners she and Warren had pur-chased for their fifteenth wedding anniversary. Two decades later, each chair bore the intaglio of its habitual sitter. Celia fit within the contours of her father's chair like a nesting doll, the imprint in its cushion foretelling the shape of things to come.

"He feels badly, you know," her mother said. She was hold-ing her wineglass by its stem, her pinky held out as if she were attending tea. Noreen, always quick to offer wine at dinner, had never invited Celia to join her in the late afternoon. It was one of the sole remaining distinctions between mother and daughter, a boundary preserved by wordless, mutual consent.

"What does Daddy have to feel bad about?" Celia asked.

"You know how it is." Noreen shrugged. "He blames him-self even when he shouldn't." She sipped her wine. "When your brother started having all that trouble, your father put a lot of stock in the fact that you turned out okay, which is why I'm so grateful that when you called last night, you didn't go into it all at once. I would have been fine, but for him, I think just hearing Djuna's name . . . You were so young when it happened and it wasn't the sort of thing we were prepared for. Not that any parent is, but we didn't know what to do."

It was quiet with the two of them sitting there and Warren asleep upstairs, the neighborhood inhabiting the afternoon lull that preceded the return of those who hadn't taken a day off work to meet their errant daughter's incoming flight.

"You wouldn't talk about it," Noreen said, "wouldn't even mention her name. Your father got his first peptic ulcer worrying about whether we were doing the right thing. We tried being casual, tried bringing it up at different times of day. We even tried bribing you to talk, but nothing worked. After a while, your father and I decided to let you start the conversation when you were good and ready, only you never did. By the time we realized you weren't going to, so much time had passed that we thought forcing the subject might only do more harm. And now, all these years later, here you are."

Late-day sun glazed the bay window. The paired recliners were angled to face a wide-screen television, bought for a more recent anniversary. Reflected in the TV's surface, Noreen and Celia looked like objects left at the bottom of a pool.

"Mommy?" Celia took a deep breath. "I think I just want to tell you this as quickly and as simply as I can."

She stopped. Her mother was shaking her head.

"Not yet," Noreen said. "It will be better for us, I think, if we have a quiet night tonight, and then tomorrow you can visit me at school."

"At school? But why?" For the second time that day, Celia

felt as if she'd been pulled from the high dive after finally having built up the courage to jump. "With Daddy asleep, can't we just . . . I mean, don't you think that this is the perfect time?" She was whining now, the sound of her indignation indistinguishable from the sound of having been denied another cookie, an extra bedtime story, the keys to the car.

"I'm sorry, sweetie," her mother said, the unfamiliar softness in Noreen's voice breaking ties with all the older battles. "But I would much rather we waited. After what happened with Jem, I learned that when certain things are said or done in certain places, it takes a long time before . . ." She shook her head. "Besides, this will finally give you a chance to see my personal office! At Christmastime the building's always closed. I think you'll be surprised at how cozy it is. It's a lovely place to have a chat. Very private, very comfortable." Her smile was equal parts apology and entreaty. "You can come in the morning, whenever you happen to wake up. I think it's best to do these things in the morning, when the day is still fresh."

Noreen touched the television remote and a moment later a snack food jingle flooded the room. At times like this, Celia's teenaged self felt like an ugly shirt she had tucked into the back of her drawer but had yet to outgrow. Whenever she came back home, her mind resumed all its worst habits: the hair-trigger sensitivities, the rush to judgment, the combative reflex that dug a dividing line between herself and the rest of the world. She partly blamed the house for her regression. Her entire childhood was contained by these rooms, her adult experience here minuscule by comparison.

- - - - - - - -

That night over the phone, Celia described all this in a degree of detail that would have bored anyone other than a lover, and which left Huck avid for more.

"What was I supposed to say?" She sighed. "So I sat with her through the end of a cable movie until Daddy woke up, and then we went to Maxi's to eat."

"You got the eggplant parm," he said. "And you all split the—"

"—the fruit de mer. And, of course, the ricotta cheesecake for dessert. With me barely able to eat because of everything Mommy had asked me not to say. We drove back with practically my whole dinner in a doggie bag, Daddy going on again about how wonderful it is that I'm home. And as soon as we were inside, the two of them went to bed even though it was only nine o'clock, leaving me downstairs, remembering."

"Tell me," Huck said.

She pictured him in their living room, worry sharpening the planes of his face. In their earliest days Celia had expected the novelty of Huck's company to be tempered by tedium, but Huck had not come into his good looks until his twenties. He had spent his acne-tormented teens becoming a good listener, sparing him the interpersonal laziness of the congenitally attractive. Celia couldn't decide if lately Huck had grown more handsome, or if she'd simply been provided more opportunities to view him at a distance.

"It's so weird," she said. "I don't understand how I've been coming back all these years without the memories jumping out at me. Djuna and I used to play Monopoly, right here in the middle of this carpet. One time—this is embarrassing, okay?—we got in a terrible fight over 'title deed.' "

"Monopoly was practically a blood sport when I was a kid," Huck said. "Those hotels were red for a reason."

Celia closed her eyes and pictured the slightly asymmetrical nose, the cowlick over the left temple, the eyes that shifted from brown to green depending on their mood—though, these days, Huck's face came to Celia most often in profile, bathed in the blue glow of the television, or sunk into a recalcitrant sleep beyond reach of the morning sun.

"Sure," she continued, "but this fight wasn't even about paying rent. Djuna was convinced it was pronounced *tittle* deed, and I knew it wasn't. We screamed about it until she finally went home. I remember I blocked the front door because I didn't want her to leave. I wanted to keep playing—I must have been winning—and finally Mommy came to the door and actually moved me aside so that Djuna could go. Later, after dinner, Djuna called to tell me that her mom said I was right. That it was *title* deed after all. I got the feeling Mrs. Pearson was on the phone along with her, making sure Djuna said it."

For a moment, they listened to each other breathe. Were she at home, they'd already be past the opening credits of a movie, Huck beside her on the couch but long gone.

"Now it's your turn to talk," she said.

"Everybody misses you," Huck replied. "At dinner, Sylvie kept sniffing at your empty chair."

"What did you eat?"

"Chili," Huck said. "Not the crappy take-out kind from Ortega's. I actually cooked."

She pictured him at the stove wielding the ancient wooden cooking spoon he wouldn't let her throw away, the dogs waiting patiently behind him.

"You're not going to let them into bed with you, are you?" she asked.

"Why, you jealous?"

She laughed. "Just guarding your welfare. They're going to be farting like crazy after all the cheese and beans I bet you fed them."

"Shit, I didn't think of that."

"You might want to keep them away during your nightly ritual. The flame might set off an explosion."

"They must still be digesting," Huck said, "because we all survived intact."

She heard it now, the slightly muted tone to his voice, like there was a bubble caught in his throat. She'd tried getting stoned with Huck, but even his connoisseurship hadn't saved her from feeling stupid and slightly paranoid. Sativa or indica, white widow or skunk, it all required her to loosen her grip on something she preferred to hold tight. Her acceptance of Huck's habit had belonged to the earliest phases of her falling in love. It felt nonnegotiable, part of the unwritten contract of their coupling, but it was impossible not to notice that what she used to liken to her mother's nightly glass of wine had lately become more like a cocktail before and after dinner.

"Did you set your alarm?" Celia asked. The first morning Huck overslept, he'd been late to school. She'd found him still buried beneath the covers, slack-mouthed and softly snoring over the clock radio when he should have been dressed, half-breakfasted, and heading out the door. The next morning, she'd intervened early enough that by eating in the car he had made it to school before the first bell. After the third day, she replaced her wake-up kiss with his name pronounced as if it were part of a larger language lesson: bed, pillow, blanket, Huck. Neither sympathetic nor accusatory, it seemed to pierce the veil of his sleep more effectively than an alarm ever could. On the four-teenth day Huck overslept, Celia decided to stop counting.

"I did," he said. "I set it to Alarm instead of Radio, and I've got the volume turned up all the way. Not that I'll need it. As long as you're gone, I'll be the girls' only option for their morning walk."

For years Celia had figured she would live alone: a small apartment in Ukrainian Village or Wicker Park shared on alter-nating weekends with a boyfriend who would have his shelf of the medicine cabinet, his bureau drawer. Their lives would sporadically intersect from Friday to Sunday, phone calls leav-ening the time in between. She had been perplexed by people who did it differently, had theorized that they were somehow less busy. In high school and college she simply had not had time to meet people. There were marches to organize and fund-raisers to plan, poems to read and meetings to attend. Her chronic overcommitment and loneliness had felt inherent, conditions like diabetes or color blindness that demanded their own concessions. Then she had met Huck.

"So you're going to visit your mom tomorrow at school?" he asked.

"She said I could come anytime after eleven."

"And before that?"

"I don't know," Celia said. "I'm going crazy thinking about it."

"I think you should take a Xanax and sleep in."

"I don't need it," she said. "I'm totally worn out. I feel like I've been awake for years."

In the silence that followed, Celia heard the sound of rhythmic breathing through the receiver. Then it faded and Celia knew that Huck had returned the phone to his ear.

"Was that Bella?" she asked. "Tell her that I miss her too."

"I love you, Ceel."

"You're my very only," she whispered. Once she had hung up, she stared at the silent phone in her hand.

She recognized what was happening to them now because it had happened once before. Six years ago, Celia's roommate had suddenly moved to Austin and none of Celia's other friends had needed a place to live. She wouldn't have been able to ask him any other way. Huck had left the apartment he'd been sharing with two other early-career teachers, and had moved into the roommate's vacated bedroom. Huck's desk was the only employed furnishing in that otherwise idle room, but Celia wouldn't let him call it his office. She maintained separate voice-mail boxes and itemized the long-distance bill, all to

avoid straining the inner mechanism that had thus far permitted this deviation from her life's previously planned course.
She'd assured Huck that these measures were not meant to
keep him at a distance but to preserve the closeness they had,
an explanation that satisfied him for a few months before he
began to drift away. Then as now, it had happened slowly, as if
he were gradually winding down. He gave up conversation in
favor of watching movies and playing guitar. He dressed for
work in stained shirts, put dishes in the drying rack that were
still encrusted with food, and tripped over Bella or Sylvie lying
in their usual places. When he had suggested that they buy their
own place, pool their savings for a down payment and apply
their signatures to adjacent dotted lines, he hadn't phrased it as
an ultimatum, but the fatigue in his voice had scared Celia
more than the prospect of saying yes. The change in him was
so gratifyingly immediate, her own relief so intoxicating, it had
been easy to convince herself that purchasing an apartment was
a solution rather than a stopgap measure. In retrospect, she saw
that the apartment had only bought them four more good
years, a grace period that had expired with the birth of Celia's
nephew. She'd thought she and Huck had become inured to
births, but then Daniel's baby pictures had arrived, showing
him with his aunt's eyes. One night, Huck asked Celia if she
wanted to go off the Pill, and she said no. He had not asked
again.

Celia realized only after she had left the couch that she
should have stayed downstairs. The guest bed stretched empty
on either side of her. The heating vent had not been opened,
and without Huck to press against, she was cold. Through the

closed windows she heard the slam of a car door from across the street, then male voices punctuated by female laughter, footfalls on the street, and finally silence.

She shifted to the edge of the mattress and, in an attempt to feel less marooned, tucked the bedding around her into a makeshift sleeping bag that recalled her first sleepovers. Mrs. Pearson had called them their bachelorette nights, Djuna's father either cloistered inside his study or overseas at one of his mathematics conferences. During his absences, Celia and Djuna were each allowed to wear one of Mrs. Pearson's negligees over their pajamas. They sipped milk from wineglasses while Mrs. Pearson drank Scotch, and stayed up watching rented videos. Mrs. Pearson's only rule was that their picks not "abound with gratuitous sex or violence." Like much of what Djuna's mother said, it was a phrase Celia had intuited more than understood. "Acclimatization," Mrs. Pearson decreed whenever she had decided that a selection rated R or PG-13 conformed to her amorphous standard. "This is the culture you live in, so you might as well get used to it. Paternalism at any age is condescending."

Most of their choices—*Freaky Friday* or *Gremlins*, *E.T.* or *The Karate Kid*—would have been perfectly acceptable to Warren and Noreen. And because Mrs. Pearson never asked Celia if she was allowed to watch movies like *Flashdance* at home, Celia was never placed in the awkward position of having to lie. She and Djuna would bookend Mrs. Pearson on the pomegranate-colored couch, an antique prettier and more comfortable than anything Celia's parents owned. Celia favored Mrs. Pearson's cocktail arm, to savor the clink of the ice. After screening something like *Blue Lagoon*, Djuna's mother would ask if Celia had any questions in the same voice that proclaimed the superiority of silk over cotton, Glenlivet over Glenfiddich. That voice took Celia for a far more cosmopolitan creature than she was, an impression Celia was loath to compromise. Her mind awash in visions of Christopher Atkins mounting Brooke Shields, she had waited until cocooned within Djuna's sleeping bag to learn how little she actually knew. Even in the darkness of Djuna's bedroom, Celia had been able make out the dolls that Mr. Pearson brought back from his frequent trips. To Celia, the international collection proved her friend's worldliness, a quality perfected by Mrs. Pearson's fingers curved around a whiskey glass. Under the dolls' collective gaze, Celia was presented with a litany of organs, orifices, and gender combinations in the blasé monotone Djuna reserved for knowledge of the highest order. Accompanying this lesson was the intimate, sweet-tinged musk of Djuna's unwashed sleeping bag, which wafted out the opening in warm puffs whenever Celia moved. This scent was as individual as a fingerprint, complex and private—the smell of a young body when it is still all smooth clefts and hollows, containing the promise of changes to come. Such cognizance was beyond Celia at the time. She had known then only that being privy to such redolence was simultaneously distasteful and thrilling, and she had attended her friend's lecture in a state of self-conscious motionlessness periodically interrupted by small, calculated gestures to assure and chastise herself with the scent's continued presence. By the following morning her nose had acclimated, the smell forgotten until next time. As Celia lay in her parents' guest bed, its fresh sheets fragrant of nothing, she elegized a green nylon sleeping bag lined with red flannel. Sometimes as she climbed inside, she had told herself that she was entering a crocodile's mouth. This was Celia's last waking memory before her mind became briefly, blessedly blank.

CHAPTER 4

Since they'd moved in together, Celia had only ever left Huck behind in order to attend an annual Midwestern audit forum, providing Huck a weekend for prog rock, late-night poker, and back-to-back Jim Jarmusch screenings during which it was understood he would smoke in the living room, subsist on pizza and Hostess snack cakes, and be unreachable by phone before noon. The number of his co-conspirators for this yearly ritual had dwindled as friends who once crashed on the couch became fathers who partook for part of one evening, then retreated along the city's commuter line to the suburbs where people like them could afford houses. Huck had always assumed that one day he and Celia would join them. When they had bought their apartment, he had imagined Celia pregnant inside it, had privately staked out the best corner for a crib. He figured they would get by until a baby turned two, at which point they'd start scouting FOR SALE signs in their married friends' neighborhoods. Given the Chicago market, a one-bedroom had seemed like a good short-term proposition. That had been four years ago.

Huck was clutching the phone as though it held some trace of Celia's voice in reserve. Bella had fallen asleep on the couch and was snoring softly, her flank warm against Huck's thigh. Were Celia here, they would be watching something noir and French on DVD and ogling Simone Signoret. Huck glanced at his guitar, but his solitude and slight stonedness—the usual preconditions for playing—were tonight undercut by a restlessness that even hydroponically grown Kush could not fix. Huck eased himself away from Bella to avoid waking her. When he stood, the couch gave a halfhearted creak, as if feigning distress at his departure. The couch was the first thing he and Celia had bought for the apartment. It was a flea-market find they'd shamelessly purchased despite a price tag well beyond their agreed-upon couch budget, and Huck wasn't sure when the creak had started, but it made him hate the couch a little each time. Some WD-40 to the springs would do the trick. This thought had been traveling with the sound, along with the word *Later*, for a long while.

They had met their senior year. Huck had been at a group reading to hear a friend, had been among maybe twenty people undergoing an evening of student poetry. One reader had blended with the next until Celia appeared at the podium. Listening to her had been like spying on someone who thinks she is alone. Huck didn't remember much about the poem itself, which had something to do with a covered bridge, but the stark sincerity with which Celia read it had caused him to turn away as if he'd been staring at too bright a light. Afterward, when he asked her out, she had smiled like she'd been offered elk or ostrich, something she'd never eaten because she'd never before thought of it as food. According to her calendar, his earliest, best chance was to meet her at Pierce Dining Hall during the forty-five minutes she allotted for dinner between classes and committee meetings. Pursuing someone with so little time turned each yes into a prize. Their first date occurred on the heels of a petition drive. Celia agreed to either food or film, but not both because she'd needed to get up early the next morning for tai chi class. During Huck's first month of courtship, each of his timely appearances at the dining hall met with the same bemused smile; each request for Celia's company was answered by the same crowded appointment book, until one institutional meal, about five weeks in, she pointed to a blocked-out portion of her Saturday afternoon and said, "How about then?" That was when Huck became regular company on Celia's weekend drives and happily abandoned the notion that he was the pursuer and she the pursued.

He loved the way his name sounded in her mouth, its sonic semblance to that other word sometimes enough to give him an erection. A chunk of his life had been spent explaining that his parents had never actually read Mark Twain. His mother was a fan of Audrey Hepburn, especially *Breakfast at Tiffany's*. Huck's name was borrowed from "Moon River" as crooned by Holly Golightly from her fire escape. He and Celia had watched the film early on, a sign—he told her later—of just how crushed-out he had been. The annual obligation of watching with his mother had turned Huck against Hepburn's Golightly, her spindly arms and feline smile too calculated for his tastes, a perfectly capable woman trying to pass for helpless girl. Celia's quiet fluency in the language of car—she was not only the best driver Huck knew, but could change her own oil, tires, fuses, and spark plugs—had been a welcome rebuttal to the Holly Golightly syndrome. Celia felt no need to brandish her skills the way some women made a production out of shooting pool or throwing a football. From the day they met, Celia had been content to be who she was. That there might be a downside to this had taken Huck years to fully comprehend.

He realized that his desire to call Celia back had less to do with anything he needed to say than with something he wanted to hear. What he had sensed that first day at the poetry reading, woven into Celia's breath, was the resolve that powered her like an inner engine. Huck discerned its undercurrents in the way she walked into a room, the way she reached for a glass, the way she leaned forward to hear what someone was saying. To Celia, the world was a place that could be fixed. She considered Huck to be a kindred spirit by default. To her, a classroom was a crucible for global betterment, every teacher a born idealist—but Huck approached his profession as a bid to slow the rate of the world's inexorable decline. While Celia insisted the difference was semantic, Huck knew that nothing short of epiphany would elevate him to Celia's rosier plane.

Theirs was a religious difference without religion, a mixed marriage without marriage. It was a disparity Huck wasn't sure he had heard in her voice just now, and its absence had unsettled him almost as much as when he'd come home the previous afternoon to find her lying across their bed in the dark.

When he'd walked through the apartment door, there'd been no reason to think that she had beaten him home, nothing to indicate a difference between that Monday and any other. Huck had taken the girls for their afternoon walk, and was coming into the bedroom to fetch a magazine. He reached his side of the bed before noticing her, the surprise of it causing him to jump as if she'd crept up from behind. "Ceel?" he'd said, as if he wasn't sure. She'd woken him that morning with the usual hand on his shoulder, his name pronounced in that way that recalled the creak of their aging couch, the sound of something that needed to be fixed. As Huck had stood over Celia in the half-light cast by the approaching dusk, he had struggled to imagine a malady dire enough to send her home from work. She'd been known to barricade herself inside her private office with herbal tea, ibuprofen, and zinc lozenges to avoid taking a sick day. Huck had considered the possibility that nursing her through some awful affliction would force an end to his late mornings, and perhaps return him to the sort of person who ministered to the slow-draining sink in the bathroom, the loose bedroom-door handle, or their beloved creaking couch. He would restore Celia to wellness, and himself to a person who did all the stuff he was supposed to do, and by the following week they'd both be their normal selves again.

But Celia hadn't been sick. They'd sat on the couch, her

body huddled against his like someone desperate for warmth. Huck hadn't been able to see Celia's face, and this had conspired with the utter incongruity of what she was saying to turn her unfamiliar. For not more than two heartbeats, Huck had found himself inhabiting a stranger's life. It was one of the most frightening things that had ever happened to him. The furniture, the dogs, the woman beside him—Huck had wanted none of it, recognized nothing. "Oh dear," he'd said, the sound of his voice bringing him back. When he had grasped Celia's chin and turned her toward him, her features were vulnerable in a way he'd never witnessed, a sight as surprising as raindrops falling up, or the ocean going still. Gone was the woman of recipes and how-to manuals, schedules and flow charts, each task reduced to its composite steps. Huck telephoned the airline himself to book their respective flights, then held Celia's hand as she'd called home. The dogs rose to their feet when Celia spoke Djuna's name, the fragility of her voice awakening a protective instinct that manifested in Huck as a faster pulse and the need to hold her close. Celia's self-reliance was such a constant that its disintegration was no less revealing than Huck's first sight of her naked, sleeping body. As they'd discussed how she should approach the coming week, Huck's solicitude had paired with Celia's uncertainty to provide a new kind of union.

Neither of them had slept that night. Smoking usually helped Huck, but Celia had lately become bothered again by his habit, so instead he had spent long swaths of time taking deep, even breaths and trying not to move. This had bestowed the single advantage of allowing him to follow her out of bed so that she hadn't needed to wake him the morning of her

flight. He'd been kissing her good-bye when he realized that it
had been weeks since they'd last had sex, and it struck him that
something was happening to them, had been happening for a
while now—a sound beneath the threshold of their hearing, a
vibration so slow and steady that it had been mistaken for stillness.

"Wait," he'd said, and watched as Celia's shoulders tensed.
The dogs had pricked their ears.

Sharing his discovery would have meant forcing her to
carry it with her onto the plane. For the next four days, it
would have occupied the empty place beside her on the mattress, casting its own imprint on the second pillow.

"I'll miss you," he had said instead, and kissed her again.
She'd smiled, and then was gone.

CHAPTER 5

At night, the tartan walls of the Scottish Suite could be mistaken for tasteful in the ambient light, which was just bright enough to allow Celia to read the titles lining the bookshelf along the far wall. This informal history of family pursuits abandoned or outgrown was arranged by topic, with sections devoted to genealogy, home maintenance, career self-diagnostics, school counseling, gardening, and fantasy baseball. A selection of guidebooks—some well-worn, others pristine, all domestic—attested to Warren's ambition to drive to all the major national parks, an aspiration he'd shelved when gas had topped two dollars a gallon. Without an actual guest beside her,

Celia felt uncomfortably aligned with the guest bedroom's cast-offs, an exile with nowhere else to go.

Her loneliness that first night magnified the foldout bed's usual discomforts, shuttling her from oblivion into hyperalertness, her brain humming with imaginary versions of all the conversations she needed to have. After a failed attempt at slow, deep breathing, Celia tried to drown her thoughts in a torrent of trivia from her most recent audits. She counted sheep by summoning scores from PepsiCo's successful vending bid over Coca-Cola. She recited the various percentages by which requests for psych-hospital beds had surpassed capacity. At some point a threshold of exhaustion was reached. Statistics beat down her mental rehearsals for the coming day until none of it sounded like language, her words denatured, her head filled with bleats and yowls.

When mid-morning angled its way through a gap in the window shade, she jolted upright, panicked that she hadn't walked the dogs. One foot was on the floor before she remembered where she was. According to her watch it was eight A.M. Her father would have left early in order to swim, but her mother's school day didn't start until nine. "Mommy?" she called, even though the stillness of the house told her she was alone. Her watch was still running on Central time.

Celia braved the hallway in her nightshirt. As children, she and Jeremy had been permitted downstairs in pajamas, but their parents only ever left the bedroom fully clothed. At some point Celia had adopted this habit, until Huck—early on in their courtship, the first demand of her he ever made—refused to serve post-coital pancakes to a woman wearing anything more than a bathrobe. The stairway carpet on the soles of Celia's feet felt like Christmas morning, circa 1981. In the kitchen, she found a note beside a fresh half pot of coffee— *Good Morning! Call me when you wake up. Love, Mom*, the office number penned beneath, as if Celia could have forgotten. Through the kitchen window, the day proceeded without her. Celia was briefly a child kept out of school. Sunlight through the hummingbird feeder stretched an illumined band of red across the table's surface. Birds were new. When Celia was growing up, her father had taken in a stray kitten, an avid hunter who—by the time Celia left for college—still had not gotten over a formative, stray-life trauma that compelled it to mewl between mouthfuls of food. A month after Howler's death, Noreen had bought the hummingbird feeder in wordless protest against the idea of adopting another.

When Celia began to dial, she realized that her mother's number did not exist in her mind as serial digits, but as a pattern her fingers tap-danced across the phone's numeric grid. Her mother picked up on the first ring.

"Good morning, this is Noreen Durst."

"Hi, Mom."

Celia had forgotten this brisker version of her mother, whose voice had overseen her daily return from middle school, marshaling the hours that separated her children's homecoming from her own. Later, that voice became the arbiter of adolescent sick days, fake and genuine, Celia's fate decided by a judge far less suggestible over the phone.

"Celie! I'm so glad you called. Did you just wake up?"

"Yeah." A smiley face beamed from the note's bottom edge. "Thanks for the coffee."

"Did you eat yet?" Noreen asked. "Everything's where we always keep it, except the cereal, which isn't in the pantry anymore. Your father moved it to the cabinet—"

"—above the coffeemaker, I know. It's been that way for years."

"Has it? Well, in the grand scheme of things it hasn't been there long. My goodness, Celie, when was the last time you called me at school?"

Through the receiver Celia heard a bell, the sound upping her pulse as if no time had passed. She checked the wall clock: second period had just begun. "That's funny," she said once the bell had stopped. "I was just wondering the same thing."

"Maybe it's the school phone line," Noreen mused, "but your voice sounds exactly like it used to. Your high school phone voice."

"Really?"

"This morning when I told Beverley that you were coming, we dusted off the yearbook from your senior year and took a look. I forgot how cramped the guidance suite used to be."

"I'm glad I finally get to see your new office."

"Not so new anymore. I got a ride with Lynne so you could have a car. She said it's no trouble for her to drive me all week."

Celia had overlooked that forgoing a rental meant depending on her parents for transportation for the first time since she'd turned sixteen.

"What time are you coming?" her mother asked.

Celia reset her watch. An hour of morning was swept away. "Would eleven fifteen be okay?"

"I told the ladies at the main office that you'd be stopping in, but you'll still need to show ID. Everything has become much more bureaucratic."

Through the receiver Celia heard the click of a door being shut. The ambient office sounds at the other end of the line ceased. Celia's mother had been cubicle-bound until the head counselor's retirement. Noreen had been dismissive of the promotion, which automatically went to the most senior employee. Most counselors stayed on just long enough to learn they wanted a different career, a process of disillusionment that lasted anywhere between one and four years.

"Celie?" she asked, as if uncertain her daughter was still there. "Did you sleep all right? Last night you looked so . . . tired. I got the feeling that your father and I had tuckered you out."

Celia was thankful there was no witness to her expression, which she'd last worn with hairspray and raspberry lip gloss.

"I slept fine, Mom. See you soon, all right?"

"There might be one hard-boiled egg," Noreen said. "Check the cold cut drawer on the left-hand side." Celia did not want an egg. After hanging up she opened the drawer. There was the egg, the very last one.

Even had Celia not spent four years remanded to her mother's place of employment, Jensenville High would have been easy to find. The school sat on a hill above the banks of the flood-prone Chenango like a giant box waiting to be filled with unwanted kittens and tossed in. It had been built in the energy-conscious 1970s, when a windowless building had seemed like a forward-thinking idea. Most people took it for a prison. On a neighboring hill, the graceful onion bulbs of the town's Eastern Orthodox church curved against the skyline with all the beauty the school did not possess. Since graduation, Celia had returned there only in her sleep.

The sight of the parking lot was both familiar and strange, like a gap-toothed former babysitter who had gotten bridgework. In Celia's day, the student lot had organized itself around Accords and Volvos that had sweetened sixteens in Jensenville's hillside neighborhood, and retooled Camaros and pickups from the floodplain side of town. The SUV had demolished these distinctions. Rarely had teenage tastes dovetailed so smoothly and universally with parental priorities, insulating car-infatuated children from their own inexperience and poor judgment with a ride guaranteed to annihilate anything it hit, scraped, or ran down.

The school building itself was utterly unchanged. A familiar sense of dread settled in Celia's belly as she approached, a reflex born of countless mornings sacrificed to its shadow. Only the front plaza was different: to the right, a bench gifted by the class of 1995 faced a bust dwarfed by its pedestal. On closer inspection, the bust—inscribed with the name William Jensen, gift of the class of 1996—was only slightly smaller than life, but the class must have spent their entire gift budget on its commission. The base was a donation, a monumental thing that turned the town founder into a pinhead. The opposite edge of the walk displayed a gray boulder the size of a crouching child. On it were carved the words JENSENVILLE HIGH, GIFT OF

CLASS OF 1993, above which hovered the school's mascot, the Jensenville Jay's wings outspread in its trademark gesture of capitulation. The rock reminded Celia of a marker designating the future resting place of herself and her former classmates, all of them to be interred beneath in eternal, obligatory reunion.

Having already funneled its students to their respective classrooms, the school's front hall was empty, its glass showcase in the same neglected spot outside the front office. Its plaques, trophies, and newspaper photos were indistinguishable from the detritus of achievement that had filled it in Celia's day. She looked at it briefly, her eyes sweeping over the faces of students whose adult trajectories would lead them either to gloss over these moments or to spend their lives pining for their return. Celia's vague recollection of the school's main office was sharpened by the wait to be acknowledged from behind its counter. Within minutes, the muscles of her face remembered its supplicatory smile. There were three desks, which seemed like two more than necessary. Celia saw a bottle of nail polish on one, a paperback on another. Forms were shuffled, phone receivers picked up and replaced in a show of busyness. Finally, as if it had only just occurred to her, the nail-polish secretary turned toward the long, narrow counter that represented the length and breadth of her domain. Once Celia had signed in, cries of "Oh, you're Noreen's daughter!" were followed by mutual visual inspections. Two of the secretaries wore the hoop earrings, acrylic nails, and hand-drawn eyebrows of blue-collar Jensenville; the third, the French manicure and gold studs of the hillside middle class. The younger two still wore their hair long, but once they hit menopause they too would go short like the secretary with hair like Celia's mother. Celia's appraisals were no less mercenary than the secretaries' raking stares. This was what high school did to people.

The older one said, "Back to visit your mom?" in a voice that evoked a smoke-damaged June Cleaver. A voice like that had logged Celia's late arrivals but she couldn't tell if this was the same one. In high school she'd never bothered to discern individuals among ambient personnel over thirty. Celia nodded, and gazes returned to desks in a collective vote of disappointment. Barring the dispatch of a behavior problem to the vice principal, it looked as though the day's highlight would be confined to lunch from the new take-out place. Without ceremony, the daughter of Noreen from Guidance was granted an adhesive tag and ejected into the hall.

Celia had arrived in the middle of fourth period. The only visible students stared out from class election posters decorating the hallway. For a portion of a portion of a second, Celia was fifteen again and late to English. Then the feeling disappeared, and she was once again a thirty-two-year-old examining homemade flyers taped to a wall. The current crop of aspiring presidents and treasurers showed the same bluster that had passed for experience when Celia was a sophomore, but with more ethnic variation. One of Celia's private embarrassments after moving to Chicago was a late-blooming awareness of her childhood's uniculture. Born to a brick monolith, she had not known to miss windows.

The school's guidance suite was at the far end of the second floor. As a freshman, Celia had climbed back stairwells to avoid passing it on her way to class. Even now, her internal awareness of the place remained her personal magnetic north. She could feel the assertion of that private compass point— lying to her left as she crossed the first-floor hallway, moving center-right as she mounted the stairs. Jensenville was small enough that a few of Celia's classmates had been the children of teachers. Celia suspected they thought she had gotten the better deal, but to her teenaged mind a teacher was less embarrassing. It was the word *counselor* that did it, binding her to a mother professionally certified to dispense advice.

The guidance suite's location above the music room had earned it carpeting. Tufted broadloom easily squelched the treble atrocity of Flute Choir—a concession to the chronic popularity of the instrument (so thin!) among dieting girls—but even deepest shag would not have muted the marching band. On rainy afternoons, or when the outside temperature dropped below 45 degrees, thumps and screeches radiated upward. The first thing Celia noticed was that brown carpet had been traded for blue. There were fewer cubicles, the school's guidance personnel having dwindled along with Jensenville's student population. Geometric lines of darker carpet color marked where the cubicles had been, a shadow grid of deeper blue compromised by fewer coffee stains and blots of trampled gum.

Celia's arrival was met by anxious glances from two girls sitting inside the door, but their faces relaxed as soon as they judged her to be irrelevant. One wall of the waiting area was given to posters eschewing drugs, suicide, and sex, the other to glossy college photos. Celia wondered if there was significance to the girls' position beneath the wall of vice.

"How can I help you?"

The guidance suite secretary asked the question in a way that did not leave Celia feeling as if she was being appraised for gossip or entertainment value, a quality Celia suspected had impressed her mother when Noreen was deciding who to hire for the job.

"Wait a minute, you must be Celia!" the secretary revised. "You're just a perfect grown-up version of your yearbook picture. I'm Beverley. You've got your mother's eyes."

On hearing the word *mother*, the heads of the girls turned.

"This lucky woman is Mrs. Durst's daughter," Beverley explained. To Celia's mortification, she found herself blushing.

"For real?" one of the girls said. At first glance, Celia thought her baby doll T-shirt spelled NUBILE in gold across the front. Celia had forgotten how pristine teenagers were—their bad habits still nascent, their bodies still indefatigable. Celia blinked. The T-shirt read NUBIAN. The girl could just as easily have been freshman or senior. Somewhere in the intervening decades, Celia had lost the ability to tell.

"Is she guiding you, like, all the time?" the girl asked.

"Not so much anymore," Celia said. She tugged at the hem of her shirt, pulling it smooth across the front, but Nubian's attention was already elsewhere, one less witness to the reappearance of Celia's high school self.

The office door that read NOREEN DURST, M.A., opened onto a room about the same size as one of the parking lot's larger SUVs. A bookcase along one wall contained the run of yearbooks marking Noreen's tenure, a collection of college catalogs, and a shelf lined with titles like *Chicken Soup for the Teenage Soul*. Celia's mother sat behind the same desk Celia remembered from the cubicle era, on which rested the same framed photo of herself and her brother from 1981. The only obvious new addition was a sealed glass cylinder containing small liquid-filled glass globes, submerged at various levels in what looked like water.

"Do you like it?" her mother asked. "It's a Galilean thermometer. Your father gave it to me I don't know how long ago, after I complained for the zillionth time about working in a windowless building. It's supposed to help me appreciate my marvelously climate-controlled environment, but mostly I just like the way it looks. Read the temperature on the lowest globe, the red one: it says sixty-eight degrees. Winter, fall, or spring—unless there's a broken duct or something—it's always sixty-eight degrees in here."

"That's good, I guess," Celia offered. She closed the door behind her and sat in the chair opposite her mother's desk, its defeated vinyl cushion collapsing beneath her.

Noreen nodded. "Different things work for different people. Ms. Tompkins actually keeps a full-size photo of a window on her wall. She's got four photos, all of the same view, one for each season. She usually changes them when you'd expect, but sometimes spring will be up when it's fall, or winter when it's spring. A few years ago when she and Dick almost divorced, it was winter for quite some time in April. She's a little cock-eyed, but they all are—therapists, I mean. She's good at what she does, better than most we've had. And she doesn't just work with adolescents—she runs a private adult practice on the days she's not here." Celia's mother made an encouraging face that Celia chose to ignore.

"Mommy, when we were talking about Djuna yesterday afternoon, you mentioned how my being so young made it hard to know what to do."

Celia paused, conditioned by yesterday's postponements to be stopped as she had before, but Noreen sat at her desk, waiting.

"What did you mean when you said that you and Daddy didn't want to do me more harm?" She understood why her mother had asked her to come. The windowless walls, the carpeting, and the closed office door created the feeling of a cloister, the world within kept separate from everything else.

Her mother sighed. "After what happened to Djuna, you got quiet. And not just about that. You used to love to talk . . . to the mailman, the doctor, your stuffed animals at naptime. When you were very little, I even recall you having a long conversation with a button."

"I don't remember," Celia said.

"It was like a tap had been turned off. No more coming home and going right into your day, or chattering about food or TV shows or the neighbors. Now you had to be asked first, and even then you didn't always answer. Your father never forgave himself, said we helped to turn you from a parakeet into a regular mute swan. Then came junior high, and all of a sudden you were busy. All those clubs and meetings. I worried at first that you were taking on too much, but your schoolwork didn't suffer and you seemed happy again. I was so grateful that I made sure not to do or say anything that might shut you back down. I suppose we should have gotten help for you back then. But at the time, I thought you were dealing with it in your own way. Kids are so resilient, and I—"

Celia shook her head. "This isn't about what you didn't do."

"But as a parent, as *your* parent, I can't help thinking about what I might have done better. You'll find this out for yourself, someday, when you and Huck—"

Celia shifted in her chair and Noreen waved her hands over her desk as if trying to dispel smoke.

"What I'm trying to say," Noreen amended, "is that even though I know it's too late, I'm ready to hear whatever you want to say."

Celia looked at her mother, unable to begin. Before she left Chicago she had thought that, having told Huck, the most difficult task lay behind her. But in the worst of all possible worlds—the one in which those she loved could not reconcile themselves to what she had done—Huck could always find somebody else.

Celia took a moment to memorize the softness around her mother's eyes and mouth. "Mommy," she said. She looked away. "I don't know how to do this."

"Sweetie," her mother said. "Oh god, sweetheart. I'm so sorry. You're being so brave, coming back to face this."

Celia shook her head. "That's not it." She took a breath. "I lied." She turned to face her mother. "I lied, okay?"

Noreen cocked her head, as if to hear better. "Darling, what do you mean?"

"I mean Djuna," Celia said, the name coming out louder than she intended. "I mean what really happened."

The room was so small, everything in it so carefully placed, that Celia felt as if she were inhabiting a shoe-box diorama.

"The man, the car," Celia said. "Djuna wasn't . . . taken."

"Of course she was, sweetheart."

Celia shook her head. "I made it up."

Noreen made a sound that was almost a laugh. "You didn't, darling. You saw it. You and Becky and Leanne and Josie."

Celia closed her eyes, opened them again. "No one saw anything because there was nothing to see. I said there was a car, and they believed me."

Celia recognized Noreen's expression from one of her early college visits home. Jeremy had come to dinner wearing headphones and sunglasses, and their mother had watched him as if he were a strange child standing too close to the street, one she was uncertain she had the authority to pull back from the curb. Noreen looked at Celia this same way now.

"That doesn't make any sense, dear," she said. "You must be confusing what happened with something else."

Celia took a breath. Over the course of countless mental retellings, the story's bones had acquired flesh. "I don't know what we were fighting about," she said. "Only that it was always like that, one of us storming off." She had told Huck with his arm draped around her like a rescue blanket, the steady warmth of him helping to lead the words from her mouth. Celia wouldn't have wanted such physical charity from her mother, but she had not anticipated the loneliness of a single, straight-backed chair. "Djuna ran into the woods fast, like it was easy for her, but where I went in, there was no clear place to walk. It was all dead branches and overgrown bushes. If anyone was going to fall, it should have been me."

After she had finished, mother and daughter sat in their respective chairs, not quite looking at each other. An art calendar pinned to the wall behind Noreen's head displayed a print of one of Monet's lily ponds. Beside it was the same poster for Cornell that had decorated Celia's bedroom until a week before her high school graduation.

"You're telling me that Djuna was hurt," Noreen began slowly. "That she fell in the woods—"

"Into a hole," Celia confirmed.

"—and that you never told anyone?"

"That's right," she whispered. She had been crying for a while, but only now noticed the tissue box at the corner of her mother's desk, placed at the perfect reach.

"Celie," her mother coaxed. "The police searched those woods. The police searched everywhere. They didn't find a thing."

"She fell into a hole," Celia repeated, because only a hole would explain the suddenness of it, the way Djuna had been there one moment and gone the next. Perhaps a ditch or some sort of abandoned well. This was adult logic, applied to childhood images belatedly remanded to her custody. This was the best that she could do. "They weren't looking for that," she explained. "They were looking for a man and a car."

"Celia, listen to me," Noreen urged, as if trying to amend a child's fear of the dark. "They searched. Everybody searched. Your father searched. I searched. We all combed every blade of grass and looked behind every tree along the road and beyond. If Djuna had been there—"

If anything, the softness around her mother's eyes and mouth had deepened. Celia could not remember the last time she had seen her mother's face so brimming with kindness.

"You don't believe me," Celia said, winded by the possibility. In all her mind's ceaseless variations of this moment, she had not imagined this.

"You were just a little girl," Noreen apologized. "A little girl forced to handle a terrible thing all by herself because her parents—" Noreen was the one crying now, her tears dampening the fabric of her blouse.

Celia looked at the glass thermometer on her mother's desk, the colored globes floating in place.

"At least with you I had the excuse that I didn't know what I was doing yet," Noreen said, shaking her head. "At least with you I wasn't in the middle of getting my degree."

"You don't believe me," Celia repeated, for herself as much as for her mother.

Noreen looked into her daughter's eyes. "I believe that's what you believe," she affirmed.

"That's not the same thing," said Celia.

"I can't believe it, sweetheart. Not knowing what I know."

"What could you possibly know?" she argued. "You weren't there!"

"Darling, do you remember talking to the police?"

Celia shook her head.

"Well, I do," Noreen said. "They came to the house, a man and a woman. There was only one woman on the force back then and she was home sick that day but they called her in because they wanted a woman to talk to you girls. They sat down with the two of us at the dining room table. They asked if you wanted to talk to them alone but you said no, you wanted me there. You'd been holding my hand from the moment you'd gotten home and you didn't let go, except to go to the bathroom and to eat. For the next month I had to sit next to you in bed, holding your hand until you fell asleep. They had some dolls and toy cars. You told them as best you could, Celie, and you weren't lying. I could always tell when you were lying because you lifted your chin and looked down your nose like you were daring me to contradict you. You weren't like that during the interview. At one point they asked you something you didn't know and you started crying because you had thought that as long as you could answer their questions, they would be able to find the man who took her."

Celia waited for her mother's words to catch on some mental corner and lift an obscuring page.

"You don't remember any of this?" her mother asked.

Celia shook her head. "I only remember what I've told you. All that I know is that I lied."

Noreen closed her eyes and massaged her temples. "You made it all up. The man, the car, the whole thing," she said, her fingers distorting the shape of her face. Celia could see capillaries through the pale skin of her mother's closed lids, thin traceries of red abutting the blue veins of her hands. "You lied to your friends, and then to me, and then to the police."

Celia nodded. She realized it wasn't sleep that made her parents look older. It was not being able to see their eyes. Eyes were the one thing that didn't gray, sag, or wrinkle; they distracted from the effects of time and gravity. With the eyes hidden, the deteriorating landscape was fully revealed.

"I'm sure part of why I can't bring myself to accept what you're telling me is that I'm your mother and I love you, but that's not the main reason." Noreen offered up a tired smile. "I was there, Celie. I'd like to think I know my own daughter."

For a moment Celia just stared, pinned by her mother's gaze. For a moment, nothing irrevocable happened. What she thought to say next seemed perfectly logical. A way to buttress her point of view.

"You didn't know your own son," Celia said, and then immediately wished she had not.

She could have added something more. There was time. Celia took scant comfort when hindsight came up equally empty in the days and weeks that followed. No number of mental repetitions produced a string of syllables with the ability to annul the power of those six words.

Silence should not have taken over. There should have been a sound to accompany the sight of her mother's face at the moment Celia beheld the extent of the injury she had inflicted, something combining the shock of a puncture wound with the permanence of breaking glass.

"I'm sorry," Celia whispered.

Noreen shook her head.

"I'm sorry," Celia repeated. "It was unfair of me. It has nothing to do with—"

"I'm sure this sounds silly to you," Noreen said quietly, "but I had this idea about myself. We all do, or maybe for you,

Celie, it's different. But for me . . . I saw what was happening
to Jem, but I didn't want to be one of those mothers who made
accusations." Her body sagged under its weight. "To accuse
your child is to rob him of so much!"

Celia touched the edge of her mother's desk. "I didn't
mean to bring this back."

"Oh you didn't, dear," Noreen said. "It never goes away.
It's been long enough that I can forget for a while, but it's like
a slipped disc or a torn knee. It never quite heals. What happened with Djuna is the same. Maybe you'll convince people
to believe what you want them to believe, but that won't
change anything for you, not in any large or helpful way."

"Mommy," Celia said.

Noreen blinked. "I'm so glad we had this talk. It's a shame
you have to go, but I'm sure you have so much to do, and—"

"I'm sorry," Celia said.

"Why, whatever for," her mother said in a way that
sounded like good-bye.

CHAPTER 6

Celia's fastest route home would have been a series of straight-aways followed by right-hand turns, three stair steps that would have brought her through the town center. Instead she traced a wide curve that held fewer memories, past buildings that had been warehouses during Jensenville's industrial zenith. One of these brick carcasses now held the town's two art galleries, divided between photorealism and abstraction, aesthetic streams contained by a single gallery until the couple running it had divorced. Celia had taken Huck there during an initial Christmas visit when she had still felt compelled to keep him entertained. Her early itineraries had provided tours of Jensenville's failed attempts at reinvention—Antiques Row, Artists'

Row, Restoration Row—until, exhausted by the town's recidivism and no longer so anxious to please, she had reverted to restaurant dinners with her parents and occasional screenings of second-run films she and Huck would never have bothered with in Chicago.

Eventually Celia reached her neighborhood's northeastern border. Her parents lived in the southwest corner closer to downtown, but Djuna had been here. Celia wasn't used to coming at the Pearsons' from this direction. Perhaps its unfamiliarity was what led her to notice the trees. During her winter visits, their bare branches disguised how much they'd grown since she was a girl. Now she saw foliage once confined to yards overarching the road in a continuous canopy of white blossoms, their petals fluttering to the street like springtime snow. Celia could not help but be impressed: she assumed trees like that had to be at least a century old. In fact, Mr. Jensen's original chestnuts had perished in a fungal blight in the 1930s. Not until the 1950s had the community association managed to pool its resources to plant flowering pear saplings where the chestnuts had once been. These were the trees that Celia saw now—trees that in ten to fifteen years would reach the end of their natural life spans. In the 1950s, the community board had wanted something economical and fast-growing. Seventy-five years had seemed like a long time. It was an open question whether Celia's parents or the flowering pears would last longer, but if Warren's health kept up, it was likely that he and Noreen would witness this final indignity, the arboreal endgame of their neighborhood's demise.

An educated guess followed by two corrective turns

brought Celia from Schiller to Handel, and the steep hill that had represented her favorite part of the bike ride to Djuna's house. After twenty-one years, all of Celia's childhood landmarks remained. Here—near the hill's base at the corner of Handel and Mendelssohn—was the blue curbside mailbox she had fed with envelopes to make it feel wanted. Here, at the midway point, was the SLOW CHILDREN sign she had taken as an insult to her pedaling speed. There, at the top, announcing the beginning of the glorious downhill ride, was the lawn that had been inexpertly replaced by rock mulch. Handel's hill was trivial to drive but on a single-speed, fixed-gear bicycle, the last few feet demanded a standing pedal. Starting from the ugliest yard in the world, Celia had coasted down Handel's far side—continuing to stand because it made her feel like Evel Knievel; and, for reasons less clear but equally urgent, singing, "Be . . . all that you can be, in the Aaaarmy," the penultimate syllable held for as long as her lungs could make it last. The sensation of the downward plunge—hair trailing like a dark pennant, eyes reduced to slits by the force of the air—had nullified the authority of good sense, debunked the doctrine of mortality. By car, Celia did not allow herself to ignore the stop sign at the base of the hill that, as a young cyclist, she had sped past, rounding the corner onto Wagner and into Djuna's driveway in a binge of forward momentum.

Unbridled speed had reinforced the sense of magical transport Celia felt each time she saw the house. The mustard yellow facade with its red and orange trim seemed like a piece of Oz bequeathed to the real world via reverse-cyclone. Mrs. Pearson had claimed that polychrome exteriors were historically consistent with the era of the town's construction and had offered, as proof, a photography book of kindred homes. The book bored Djuna, but Celia had imagined each house as her own. Years later, after she left for college, a polychroming fad had flared among the more ambitious of the neighborhood boosters, some of whom acquired community improvement grants and fostered notions of a Jensenville Painted Lady District inspired by the famous homes of San Francisco. Enthusiasm had faded with the first paint jobs, which were no match for East Coast winters. Though a few stalwarts still enlivened the neighborhood like trees in perpetual autumn, Celia's arrival onto Wagner Street showed that Djuna's was not among them. Celia pulled over, her chest constricting. It had been ridiculous to think the colors would have survived. The thrill of turning a certain corner, restored after twenty-one years, was demolished by the sight of a white facade with brown trim.

According to the unadjusted time on her cell phone, it was Huck's planning period.

"Finally," he said.

"Is this an okay time?" she asked. She gaped at the plain house like it was on fire.

"I've been sitting here with the phone lying between my grade book and my third-period essays on Manifest Destiny and Mission," he said. "How did it go with your mom?"

Celia could not stop staring. She tried to project the colors from her memory, but nothing would stick.

"Sweetheart," Huck said. "You're crying."

"I made a detour on my way back," she said. "I don't know why, but I thought it was a good idea."

"Ceel, where are you?"

"At Djuna's."

"You sound so sad."

She looked around. There—in that narrow strip of grass between houses, beside a gray electrical box the size of an industrial freezer—she could almost see the girls they once had been. She remembered crouching with Djuna, out of breath from running, between them a library tote filled with whatever food they had filched from the kitchen on their way out the door. The steady hum of the electrical box was imperceptible unless you were right next to it, and became downright ominous when you placed your ear to its metal side. Because they'd never seen anyone else there; because they'd discovered the sound for themselves; because their friendship thrived on such exclusive mutual possessions, they decided they were the only ones in the world who knew the box's secret. They alone had managed to evade its net of inaudible sound waves, designed to prevent everyone else in the neighborhood from wanting to leave. At age eleven, Celia and Djuna had been old enough to ride their bikes wherever they wanted, and to pocket keys to their respective homes. They'd taken their first steps into the hugeness of the universe beyond, and found each other. The grass around the electrical box formed a long, untended zone that no one else had claimed. To crouch there was to become invisible. For Celia, the best moment was when they first arrived, each grasping one of the tote bag's handles, a single creature composed of four ready legs and two synchronous hearts. Whenever she agreed to the game, it was for this moment of union, the strongest alliance she'd experienced outside the inherited bonds of family, and the most powerful, vulnerable thing she knew. Her fun lay in skulking behind bushes and evading imagined pursuers while gorging on commandeered cornflakes and chocolate-covered raisins, but Djuna talked of Greyhound buses to New York City, and of money her mother kept in a bureau drawer. After exhausting their supplies while arguing over destination behind a series of trees and parked cars, they invariably returned to Djuna's, an endgame Celia treated as a private victory every time.

Driving back along Schubert, Celia passed two joggers in matching sorority T-shirts, identical ponytails bobbing behind them. Across the street, a student tenant sat enthroned upon his lawn's recliner. He listened to his iPod, his head bobbing at a more frantic tempo than the jogging sorority sisters, an open textbook resting on his lap. When Celia exited the car, he briefly looked up before returning his gaze to the book, abandoning Celia in mid-wave, her mouth having assumed the reflexive neighborly smile. It was further proof that she was getting old, this allegiance to etiquette abandoned by the younger generation. Once upon a time, her own parents had scolded her for not saying hello. Soon, even eye contact would be discarded. All pretense of community would be extinguished.

Celia opened the front door with the same key she'd always used, the one she never failed to bring back east. Between the fake rock and her parents' spares she knew there was no chance of being locked out, but Celia had owned this key for two-thirds of her life. It had survived the era of lost umbrellas, hats, and retainers. It bore the stamp of a hardware store that had

burned down under suspicious circumstances around the time
she was learning to drive. In some future Celia hesitated to
imagine, her parents actually would move and the key would
be thrown away or consigned to a jar of orphaned objects—
but for now, it slid in and turned without a hitch. Not all keys
did: this one had been well-made. It was not Celia's house anymore, but each time she turned this key in the lock, it became
her house again.

She entered the den before remembering that the computer had been moved to her brother's old room, opposite hers
at the far end of the second floor. Celia took the stairs slowly,
noticing for the first time that years of direct sunlight from the
front hall had blanched the pine carpeting to pale green. She
hadn't spent much time in Jeremy's room beyond putting him
to bed as his conscripted babysitter. Before she'd left for college, her brother had been an uncomplicated creature of navy
blue Converse and cargo pants, a boy who smelled of peanut
butter. His room had held no allure, its secrets either outdated
or irrelevant. Warren had talked of wanting a home office, but
Celia suspected the computer's relocation had more to do with
trying to rid the place of its ghosts. According to Noreen, Warren had been the one to find him. He had needed to let himself in—the only detail Celia had been told, but it was enough.
The house had been built before the invention of doorknobs
with push-button locks. The keyhole of each interior door had
been unsexed long ago by the loss of its key. It was impossible
to know whether or not her parents' pathological respect for
privacy had predated their habitation of a house with unlock-
able doors, but even in grade school, when night frights had

sent Jeremy screaming awake, Warren's headlong rush for his son's room had always stopped at the threshold. Knocking, he would say, "Jem, it's Dad. Is it okay for me to come in?"

All that was visible from her brother's doorway was the computer desk and the bookshelf on the wall just beyond the door's reach. Crossing inside, Celia wondered whether she was walking over the spot where her brother had collapsed. The replacement carpet contrasted oddly with the rest of the room, which was a ravaged time capsule. Only the least coveted artifacts of childhood remained—uncherished books and unloved toys, unprized awards and souvenirs from unmemorable vacations. Beside a dust-choked field day medal sat the carapace of a plaster arm-cast covered in faded signatures. Next to that, the relevant Jensenville High yearbooks, bought reflexively by Noreen each year when purchasing her own. Jeremy's were fuzzed with dust, their spines unbroken. Thumbtacks memorializing the dimensions of discarded posters were interspersed with spackled wall patches, none smaller than the width of a fist. The ceiling was dotted with a few persistent glow-in-the-dark stars that had long outlasted their constellations.

Warren's computer monitor displayed a more recent photo of Daniel than the one on the coffee table downstairs. It was a candid shot that Jeremy or Pam must have taken since last Christmas, because he was wearing a sweater Celia remembered him receiving. Her nephew was napping on a couch, looking more like his father than ever. Asleep, Daniel sucked his thumb just as Jeremy had; he had the same thick eyebrows and—Celia wasn't sure why she'd never noticed it before—the same oblong mole in the center of his left cheek. Daniel would turn two in June. Though Celia was kept up-to-date by the photos Pam faithfully posted online, last Christmas was only the second time she had seen him in person. Daniel's boundless enthusiasm for motion and collision did not remind Celia of Jeremy in particular. She had witnessed it in enough of her friends' children to know it was the province of small boys. What struck Celia most about young children was the intensity of their passions, life too new to be modulated, perspective a possession not yet acquired. At that age friendship was a continuous present based on proximity and the shared fact of being alive. Heartbreak and betrayal were commonplace, authentic and ardent each time, forgotten within moments.

Celia stared at the computer screen, willing herself to begin. All she had to go on were their names at age eleven: Rebecca Miller, Jocelyn Linke, Leanne Forrest. Less than a decade ago seeking them out would have required, at the very least, the cultivation of a reference librarian or a local archivist, perhaps even a private investigator. Now all Celia needed was broadband access. Of the three, only Rebecca's name was hopelessly generic. Celia started with Josie. What had once been fodder for countless noir movies had been reduced to typing a name and clicking on a button that said Search.

There was just one. The hits were all related, all having to do with art. Jocelyn Linke had kept her name. Celia stared at the monitor, stunned by how easy it had been.

A gallery Web site provided a bio. Place and date of birth were all the confirmation Celia needed, the only information she recognized. After college in Wisconsin, Josie had attended the Art Institute of Chicago. The year Celia started working

for the Auditor General, Josie had been seven blocks away finishing her MFA. They might have ridden the same El train,
eaten the same weekday lunch specials. Back when she'd
known Josie, everyone was artistic, life a steady accretion of
paintings and stories, lopsided clay animals and braided friendship bracelets. Josie's people had looked like people, her trees
like trees, but no more or less than anybody else's. She had
become the sort of artist Celia didn't have a name for, the kind
who did a bit of everything. Thumbnail images of Josie's paintings, sculptures, and installations lined the bottom of the screen,
each in turn filling the upper portion in a cycling slideshow.
All the images depicted women and girls in various configura-
tions, but three made Celia flinch. She had been anticipating a
search that would take days, a mental road trip that would provide her time to prepare for seeing the people she had pushed
to her memory's margins. Instead, as if delivered by supersonic
transport, here were Josie's monogrammed glasses, Becky's
narrow-set eyes, and Leanne's broad forehead, details Celia's
mind had elided but which were as native to her as her own
scent. Their familiar faces sat atop fanciful bodies that sprouted
bells, scales, or thorns. The first piece showed the five of them
on the march, their girl bodies tapering into duck feet below
the knees. Celia and Djuna led the procession, their heads perfectly aligned, Celia by now having permanently adopted the
good posture she had once disdained. Josie and Becky flanked
Leanne, whose arms were crossed to form an X as if frozen in
the middle of a walking version of a hand game—*Miss Mary
Mack, Mack, Mack/All dressed in black, black, black*. Except for
Leanne, intent on her game, they were all smiling.

The second image showed Celia and Djuna frozen in mid-argument, their legs rooted to the ground. Their bodies had been transformed into prickly plants leaning toward each other as if bent by opposing winds. Celia could feel the memory of her sneer in the muscles of her face, recalled the way her jaw would ache afterward.

She couldn't bear to look at the last piece for more than a few moments. Djuna sat with her face averted, her seated body a network of gauges gone haywire, their needles all in the red. Josie watched from a distance, her head attached to a body of peepholes, while Celia stood with her back to Djuna not more than one arm's length away. Celia's body was frozen in escape but her head was turned fully around, owl-like, to stare at Djuna from a 180-degree angle. Celia felt as though the contents of her mind's most protected corner had been rifled and put on display. The scene Josie had re-created was proof that at least one person already knew what Celia had come back to say.

The gallery didn't provide any contact info aside from its own. Celia spent half an hour traveling from hit to hit along the information highway looking for a personal phone number or an e-mail address before noticing her brother's old push-button telephone, waiting all this time at the edge of her vision. She went downstairs to consult the White Pages. It had been years, but her parents kept the phone book in the same place they always had, in the magazine rack beneath the phone handset that, in the pre-cordless era, had endowed that corner of the den with special powers. Celia didn't think the apartment in Chicago even contained a telephone directory, remembered

annually ignoring the stoop-side appearance of each new edition, so deracinated by the rise of the cell phone that it had
become no more desirable than a Chinese take-out menu.

The listing for Ron and Sandy Linke was nestled between
Lin and *Linker*. Celia had never visited Josie's house but
remembered the sight of the corner street sign outside the bus
window, and Josie's pronunciation of Mozart Street as if refer-
ring to art owned by a guy named Moe. The afternoon bus
provided Celia and Djuna the day's best opportunity to wield
their power, its two- and three-seaters enforcing a much
stricter pecking order than any lunchroom table. They'd
choose a three-seater, using their backpacks to fill the extra
space until the bus lurched into motion, at which point they'd
remove their bags to reveal the available seat, fifth-grade
Salomes executing their own Dance of the Seven Veils. They
ignored Becky and Josie's nearby two-seater, except on the days
they invited Becky to join them at Djuna's house to play. On
those occasions, Becky would sit between them, leaving Josie
stranded across the aisle. As Josie's stop neared, she would open
a book and pretend to read, never turning a page. Celia
remembered the deliberation with which Josie would hoist her
book bag and then check her seat, feigning deep interest in
ensuring she had left nothing behind, hesitating until the bus
driver threatened to make her walk from the next stop if she
didn't get a move on, forcing Josie to accept that she was not
going to be invited too. "Call me," she would say each time
she left the bus. They never did.

Mrs. Linke recognized Celia's name, told her she was sure
Josie would be thrilled to hear from such a good old friend.

She would get back to her with contact information; Josie had so many different phone numbers these days, she was never sure which one to give. Celia expressed thanks and hung up, her hands shaking. She had forgotten Mrs. Linke until she'd heard the slight Southern drawl. Josie's mother had been a frequent field trip chaperone and classroom helper, a tirelessly upbeat woman in long, flowing skirts and scoop-necked blouses, whose equally fervent praise of tangled cursive exercises and perfect math worksheets confounded any nascent impulse toward self-pride. Though the same sugared voice had greeted Celia on the phone, Mrs. Linke had skipped the What-do-you-dos and Where-are-you-nows that were the standard parlance of old friends' mothers. This former enthusiast for anything remotely related to her daughter had not wanted to know anything more about Celia than she already did.

Celia tried to turn her attention to the two friends who remained. For most of her elementary school career, Leanne had been no more than a February obligation, hers a remnant valentine after the best had been apportioned from the pack. Leanne had ridden a different school bus, and Celia's memory was powerless to retrieve a phone number she was certain she had never dialed, but she thought she'd called Becky's old number often enough to pick it from a list. Celia scanned the listings, a wilderness of Millers. She recalled a rough-barked tree with aboveground roots, a rainbow painted on a bedroom wall, a Jewish menorah and wineglass on a living room shelf, but she couldn't recall where the house had been, and no numeric sequence caught her eye. Then she remembered: Becky's parents had divorced. This had been in middle school, the news coming to Celia as third-hand gossip in the cafeteria line. Mrs. Miller had been a trim woman with cropped hair who joked about her clumsiness, Mr. Miller a sharp-nosed man to whom Celia was always "Miss Durst."

Upstairs at the computer, Celia typed Becky's and Leanne's names into a people-finding Web site that produced too many potential listings for Becky, but a single listing for a Leanne Forrest of the right age, living one town over. For $14.95, Celia was supplied with street and e-mail addresses. It was all horrifyingly easy. As Celia labored over a suitable message to send, a memory of Leanne returned to her, summoned by the motion of her fingers. Celia remembered a recess jump rope taken from the blacktop and dragged to the edge of the soccer field for an impromptu lesson in knots after Djuna had demanded that Leanne prove she was good at something. Leanne had handled the rope with shy assurance, her short fingers beautiful as they looped it around.

"This is a bowline," she had explained in a soft voice at odds with her confident hands. "It's good because it doesn't slip or jam. You can tie it to pretty much anything you want to hold on to. Then there's the square knot?"

As she tied it, Djuna had scowled. "Everyone knows that one."

"Oh," Leanne apologized, finishing it quickly before making it disappear. "Well . . . then maybe this one?" She crossed the rope once, then again over itself and through a loop before pulling it tight. "It's called a figure eight." Leanne surrendered it to Djuna for inspection, infinity on a string. "I've got a friend

who's a Boy Scout. They get to do this stuff all the time."
Leanne had eyed the rope as if it were a delicious food.

"Cool," Djuna had proclaimed, pulling the knot at either
end. When they'd returned to class, Djuna had allowed Leanne
to fill Celia's usual spot beside her for the walk back. Celia had
been jealous even as she'd known she was witnessing something
too rare to covet, like a double rainbow or a summer hailstorm,
a fleeting moment of grace that would end as inexplicably as it
had begun.

CHAPTER 7

The sound of the front door carried upstairs and froze Celia's hands at the keyboard. Her mother's arrival could only be awkward, their morning encounter tainting the space between them. Family conflicts were less often aired than suffocated, civility heaped upon civility until the trouble was smothered under the accumulated weight of so much decorum.

"Cee Ceee-ee, I'm ho-ome!"

The certainty of her mother's arrival briefly made Warren a stranger. *There's a man here*, Celia thought, and then realized it was her father. As a girl, she would have run to his outstretched arms shouting, "Daddy! Daddy!" Relief might have tempted her to do the same now, had she been less familiar with her father's schedule. He should still have been on campus. From the top of the stairs she saw that his hair, unlike her mother's, was as thick as it had ever been.

"Aren't you early?" she asked.

"The registrar's office on a Wednesday afternoon is not a very busy place." He grinned. "Your mother's been delayed. We can get takeout or there's a casserole in the freezer."

"Won't she be home for dinner?"

Warren shrugged. "She said she wouldn't be back in time to get it started. What appeals?"

"Casserole is fine." Celia examined her father's face, looking for clues. "Did she sound—okay?"

"Oh, sure," he said. "She feels terrible about having to miss out, but I guess there was an incident with one of her students and a conference was arranged at the last minute. She sends her love."

He looked away, and that was how Celia knew that her mother had told him everything.

She was losing her touch: once, she wouldn't even have needed her father to turn. Life with Huck had impaired her family fluency, dulled her eye for the slight tightening of muscles around the mouth. The subtle cadences of uncertainty, embarrassment, and avoidance had blurred to her unpracticed ear. She and Huck had almost broken up over his obliviousness to such subtle syntax. A certain glance accompanying a "No, nothing's wrong" meant nothing to him. He was blind to the difference between an obliging and an assenting smile. Huck raised his voice in his defense; he spoke without first weighing his words. According to him, these were perfectly acceptable ways to communicate and not, as Celia had been raised to think, the vocal equivalents of public frontal nudity.

By the time she joined her father downstairs, he was putting away his coat. They hesitated at hugging distance.

"So," he said, patting her shoulder. "What have you been up to?"

Kissing his cheek, she encountered delicate skin, soft like a dried peach. Celia felt side-swiped by a sign of aging she had not anticipated, her father's face gone fragile.

"Mostly searching the Internet," she said. "Typing in names, seeing if I can find where everyone's gone."

"Any luck?"

"A little."

Warren nodded. "Glad to hear someone's putting that machine to good use."

During a performance audit of a V.A. rehabilitation program, Celia's team had discovered a cache of fancy new computers that had been left uninstalled, the V.A. staff still relying on ancient, slow contraptions that ran off floppy disks. The guy assigned to teach the new system had moved to California. One of Celia's biggest challenges was to word her findings in ways that didn't sound punitive, an exercise in euphemism for which her family life had left her uniquely prepared. *New equipment is underutilized*, Celia had reported. *Personnel would benefit greatly from training and initiative.*

Celia trailed her father into the kitchen, their reflected profiles darkening the portraits on the photo wall like passing clouds. "Lately we've been talking about redecorating that room for Daniel," he said. "A fresh coat of paint, some new curtains, toys on the shelves."

Since finding Josie's mother in the local directory, Celia had been carrying her cell phone in her pocket. Each time she moved her leg she felt the phone shift and thought, _Now_.

"Does Mommy stay late often?"

Her father opened the freezer and retrieved a baking dish opaque with frost. "Not so much, but she never says no. There's a guidance counselor award the school nominates her for every year. Some sort of national recognition. She's never won, but just the nomination itself is something, don't you think?"

The casserole thudded against the counter, a frozen brick of food. Warren eyed it warily. "I think it's great the way you and Huck trade off in the kitchen," he said. "I mean, I'd call your mother and myself pretty modern for our generation, but it's not like you two, or Jeremy and Pam for that matter. Your brother was so wonderful when Daniel was born—doing the laundry, cooking the meals. Made me realize how useless I'd been to your mother when you two came along." He flashed the same grin that apologized for speeding tickets and forgotten errands, a smile somehow both contrite and proud.

"It's awfully nice," Celia said, "their offering to come all this way on Saturday, especially with Pam pregnant." Her brother lived an hour's drive northwest on Route 79, in a house newer and uglier than their parents', a modest Cape Cod with vinyl siding that was set back from the road. For the same money, he could have gotten something older and prettier in town but Jeremy had wanted land. Enough trees edged the property to block the sight of the neighboring houses, which were beyond shouting distance on either side. Her brother's happiness there was the latest in a lifelong series of proofs demonstrating their differences.

"Well, that's Jeremy for you," Warren said. "I sleep easier knowing he's so close. I never would have figured him for a country mouse, but then again I thought Chicago was just a stage for you, so I guess I'm oh for two." He shrugged. "The older I get, the less I mind being wrong. As it turns out, life gets a lot more relaxing once you decide you don't know a damn thing about it."

"Daddy, what do you remember about Djuna?" Celia asked.

Her father's features retracted like a frightened snail's, and he turned to busy himself with the casserole and the microwave. Considering that Warren had grown up Catholic-schooled in a family of brothers, he had done an admirable job of father-ing a female firstborn, but not even in the terrible months sur-rounding Jeremy's detox did he worry for his son with the same grandiloquence. No return trip from Jensenville was complete without his phone call to confirm that Celia had arrived safely in Chicago. Her freshman year had birthed her father's first bleeding ulcer—his body's retort to being denied the chance to drive to his daughter's aid at any moment. Celia hadn't been informed until his release from the hospital, where he'd gone after vomiting blood. Her will to sound the depths of his anxiety was matched by his capacity for silence.

"Djuna was a real spitfire," he said. "She told me once that I should go on business trips. Said you'd love me more if I went away and then came back." He shook his head. "She was will-ful, that girl. Once she decided to do something, there wasn't any stopping her."

He lifted his chin and cleared his throat, and Celia realized that whatever he was about to say had been practiced, perhaps even first written down. "You and me, Cee Cee, we're num-bers people. Your brother too." He gauged Celia's face for something he didn't seem to see. "Heck, one of the main rea-sons I have a hard time thinking about retirement is that work is one of the few places I can be absolutely certain of anything. I mean, there's always Sudoku but that's not the same thing, is it?" His brow furrowed. "We're people who like our lives orderly," he asserted. "We like to know what we can rely on and what we should toss out. And when you're told something that goes against almost everything you've come to believe about a certain subject, or a certain person—"

At the sound of the front door swinging open Warren called out, "Norrie?" like a man about to burst into song.

When Celia's mother appeared in the kitchen doorway, relief waxed Warren's face smooth. Differently timed traffic lights or a backup on Main Street, and Celia would have been subjected to her mother's opinion all over again, dressed in her father's voice.

"Hello, you two," Noreen said, as if she'd arrived at a din-ner party. "It looks like I lost a bet with myself. I was sure you were going to get Chinese." She laughed in Celia's general direction.

"You're just in time to join us," Warren said. "We're mid-defrost."

"Actually," she chirped, "I'm going to go straight to bed. I was chin-deep in student assessments for five hours and I'm just so tired."

"Would you like me to bring you a plate?" Warren asked.

"No thanks," she demurred. "I ate a little something on my way home."

"I'll be up soon," he promised.

She shrugged. "Whatever you like, dear. I'm sure I'm going to be out the minute my head touches the pillow." It was seven thirty.

"Mommy?"

Her mother had retreated halfway down the hall. "Yes?"

"Good night," Celia said, the word hanging between them like a limp sail.

"Good night, Celia." For a moment it seemed that someone might say something more, but then no one did.

CHAPTER 8

It was waiting for Celia the next morning, the half-familiar name sitting in her in-box in bold type:

From: Lee Forrest
To: Celia Durst
Subject: Re:

Celia—Of course I remember you. If you'd e-mailed me a few years back, I probably would have deleted your name along with the porno spam. And as much as I believe in second chances, if an envelope with your handwriting had come to me through the

regular mail, I guarantee that thing wouldn't have
made it past my front door.

I went to that people Web site and typed in a bunch
of names I haven't thought of in a while. They were
all there waiting for me, which just goes to show
that if someone isn't in touch these days it's not
because they can't find you. But it doesn't surprise
me that you couldn't track down Becky. She
traded in Rebecca Miller for Rivka Rosentraub
about fifteen years back. A lot has changed since
she and I were in touch, but I've got an old number
for her in Scranton that I'm betting is still good.
(570) 790-0172. If she answers, tell her I say hello.

I'm not going to call like you asked and I don't want
you calling me. E-mail is all you're going to get, so
make the best of it.

—Lee

When Celia had sent her message into the void, it had felt
more séance than summons, her keystrokes so many table rap-
pings to conjure a long-lost voice from the ether. Once her
pulse had returned to normal and her grip on the chair had
loosened, she read and reread Leanne's words, searching for
echoes of the girl who had trailed their small group like a late-
day shadow. Leanne hadn't worn their clothes, or earned their
grades. One day they had arrived to find her at their regular

lunch table, already eating. On the second day she was waiting with a four-leaf clover she had sealed up in clear tape, and on the third with an old Wheatback penny. Djuna had accepted each offering as if it was her due, and on the fourth day Leanne handed each of them a perfectly smooth, tumbled stone.

"Can I join?" she'd asked.

"Join what?" Djuna replied for them.

"Your club."

Celia was surprised by the word, but Djuna rolled her eyes as if this were a tedious question. "Give one reason we should let you," she demanded, as if the club were not something Leanne had just called into being.

Leanne shrugged and looked away. "Because you took my stuff?"

"So?" Djuna made a gesture that encompassed Leanne's lank hair, her button-down shirt with the frayed collar, the bell-bottom corduroys that should have been straight-leg, their ridges worn away at the knees. "You're not like us."

"Could you teach me?" Leanne's voice had gone small.

With that, they ceased to be girls who happened to swap desserts from their lunch boxes, or who casually maintained tandem perches atop the parallel bars at recess. Leanne's desire required them to determine what made them desirable. One week they wore colored shoelaces; the next, only white would do. Each day became a new opportunity to demonstrate the value of their company, to prove their facility for cool. If Leanne was tested most often, it was only because she was so willing. Leanne showed them just how far they could go.

Celia reread the e-mail, and pictured Leanne's solemn face.

When she reached Becky's name, she stopped. She had imagined Djuna's disappearance as a scattering explosion. That Leanne had stayed in touch with anyone was surprising enough, but a friendship with Becky seemed as unlikely as the Scranton telephone number. Where Celia had been accustomed to A's, Becky had expected perfect scores, the freak occurrence of a B-plus once reducing her to tears. Celia would have put Becky Miller somewhere with an identifiable skyline and an international airport. If Leanne's information was good, Becky was only an hour away. Celia was dizzied by the prospect of two of her quarry within such close reach. She replied to Leanne first to give Becky enough time to get to work, preferring to dial when it seemed most likely she'd reach a machine. She wanted to temper the surprise of her reappearance to guard against scaring her old friend away. A woman's voice answered on the third ring.

"*Shalom?*"

"Hi, um, I think I have the wrong number." Celia thought of all the times she picked up the phone in Chicago to be met by a torrent of Spanish. "I'm looking for Rivka Rosentraub?" She began crossing out the number she had written down.

"Speaking."

Celia dropped her pen. "Oh! I'm sorry, is this Becky? I mean are you—were you—Rebecca Miller?"

There was a pause.

"Who is this?"

"Celia Durst? I knew Becky when she was a girl."

They had known each other since first grade, when Becky skipped kindergarten and was placed in Celia's class, but they had not become friends right away. Becky's friends were ones she chose for herself, their acquisition as deliberate as the cuffs on her pants and the part in her hair. She had tapped Celia in third grade.

"Celia? Is it really you?"

Celia heard footsteps through the receiver. Music that had been audible ceased. She remembered an afternoon spent in Becky's living room, moving unselfconsciously to the more danceable tracks of *Free to Be You and Me*.

"Is this Becky Miller?" Celia asked again.

"Yes, of course! Hello, Celia! Forgive me if I sound startled. This is a bit unexpected."

"I'm sorry," Celia said. "I got your number from Leanne."

There was a pause and a sharp inhalation of breath, followed by a long exhale.

"Did you really?" The voice chuckled. "*Yasher ko'ach*. How is she? How is Leanne?" It was a matter-of-fact voice, good for relaying driving instructions or bad news.

"Good!" Celia chirped. "Actually, we didn't talk or anything. I found her online. She was kind enough to give me your number."

"You were looking for me in particular?"

"No," Celia said. "I was looking for all of us. I mean—"

"I know what you mean."

Another exhale. The sound of a cigarette being smoked. "How have you been, Celia? It's been, what—twenty years?"

Celia detected a rasp, wondered if it came from the cigarettes. It was a sound that bore no relation to her mental image of Becky, a picture hopelessly out-of-date.

"That's right," Celia said. "I live in Chicago now."

"So far away. Are you married?"

"I'm not."

"So, no children." It was not a question. "I have seven. Chaya, my oldest, turned eleven last summer. Seeing her at that age made me think of things I hadn't thought of in a long time. And now the phone rings."

Becky was spared the sight of Celia gaping into the phone.

"Celia? Are you still there?"

"Yes. Sorry, Becky. Rivka—"

"You can call me Becky. Rivka, Rebecca. It's the same name."

"Becky."

Seven. Celia was consumed by mental images of *The Waltons*, a cigarette inserted between Olivia Walton's fingers. "Um, I know it's odd hearing from me like this, but I was wondering if we could meet."

In the pause that followed, Celia cursed her eagerness, half expected to hear a click followed by silence.

"Is this some sort of alumni thing?" Becky said. "I'm not really the class reunion type."

"No, that's not it. I'm . . . I happen to have business in Scranton"—it was too late for Celia to begin again—"and it'd be great . . . Is there any chance that we could have lunch?"

"You're going to be in Scranton?" Becky's laugh—a low stutter like a child's imitation of a car engine—was unchanged. Celia's non-phone hand reflexively rose in greeting, as if she had just spotted her friend across the room.

"*Bashert* is *bashert*: it must be fate. Of course we can meet,"

Becky agreed. "Any time is good so long as we can meet after eleven and before one thirty."

Celia checked her watch. If she left immediately, she could be there by noon.

"I can be there anytime after twelve fifteen."

"Then let's meet at Blum's at one. Do you know the area?"

"No."

"I'll give you directions."

Celia had a fleeting memory of a younger but equally concise voice playing at choreographer inside a living room with green shag carpeting. She remembered a gray velour armchair beside a spindly-legged side table holding a plate of carrots and American cheese singles that the two of them raided in between performances.

She had just enough time to shower and dress. Her mind was blank as she got herself ready, quieted by the shock of her imminent meeting. As she left the house, her footsteps echoed on the front walk, the street empty, the neighborhood still. Any small delay risked annulling Becky's substantiation. Noreen's car had always been the only one Celia and Jeremy were permitted to drive. Warren's was off-limits even to his wife, their sole unshared possession. During Celia's junior year at Chicago, Jeremy had totaled the Japanese compact in which Celia had earned her license, a car the color of a ripe banana that Celia had christened the Monkeymobile. The loss of that car, Celia's first and only stick shift, had affected her more than the death of the family cat. She had never adapted to her mother's subsequent string of sedate sedans, still found her foot pining for a clutch that wasn't there.

Jensenville lay along the shim of land that kept I-81 from the Chenango, the highway wooing the river into Pennsylvania before abandoning the chase. Scranton was a straight shot south. Celia associated the interstate with the fireworks sold across state lines, remembered high school parties that had featured bottle rockets or Roman candles purchased in Great Bend and smuggled seventeen miles back north. She ignored a recumbent gas gauge to speed her departure. While breathing the fumes at the first self-service station across the Pennsylvania border, she was gripped by the idea of heading east and making for one of the oddly named towns nestled within the wooded bends along the river. She briefly imagined calling Huck from Cahoonzie or Equinunk and asking what he thought of starting over in a place that held no history for either of them.

For fifty-three miles, it didn't occur to her to turn on the radio, the thrum of her own thoughts carrying her from exit 230 to exit 191. Blum's Dairy Restaurant was located in Scranton's northern outskirts, tucked inside a strip mall between a maternity outlet and a bakery that announced itself in English and Hebrew. Between judicious speeding and light traffic, Celia had arrived with forty minutes to spare. She dialed Huck, but hung up when she reached his voice mail. Chicago seemed like the other side of the world. She decided she might as well be seated when Becky arrived, sensed her old friend might have a better chance of recognizing her than the other way around.

A crowded deli counter stretched away from the door, the wall behind it a periodic table of bagels.

"Number Fifty-one!" a broad-shouldered voice bellowed from inside a fraying apron.

The woman who held up a ticket and gestured toward the counter was indistinguishable from the others placing orders or awaiting their turns, all of them wearing full-length skirts and precisely modeled hair. The studious way they avoided looking at Celia was proof she had been noticed, proof it wasn't her imagination that clothes unremarkable everywhere else here looked risqué.

She must have been standing inside the door for some time because the spindle-fingered man behind the register, who had not spoken a word while ringing up the steady stream of customers, finally glanced in Celia's direction.

"You've got to take a number," he said in a way that showed he couldn't tell whether she was hard of hearing or mentally impaired.

"I'm sorry, I'm not—" she began.

He gestured to the left. "Dine-in over there."

Celia turned, and for the first time noticed a door leading to a small dining room. The room was plain but clean, with plastic checkered tablecloths covering the tables, each anchored by a small vase containing a single artificial flower. Aside from a few men in dark fedoras and dark suit jackets, the tables were occupied by the same kind of women crowding the deli counter. Celia was unmistakable, a jay among puddle ducks.

The waitress seated Celia at a small table along the inside wall, hidden from the door and away from the front window. Celia explained that she was waiting for someone, and ordered matzoh ball soup. She owed the sum of her Jewish expertise to a single bar mitzvah attended in middle school. She and David Lupinsky had been in Olympics of the Mind together. She hadn't known he liked her until she'd accepted his invitation, and then learned he hadn't asked anyone else from their team. She'd bitten the inside of her cheek to avoid falling asleep during the service, and then danced with David for two slow songs before spending the rest of the party hiding in the bathroom. When David's mom had come to check on her, Celia had accepted two Advil for cramps she didn't have, along with a mini-pad she was certain she had misapplied to her underwear in a way that would broadcast her bluff to every woman in the Howard Johnson's banquet hall. In a panic, she had torn the thing in half and divided it between the cups of her training bra, the only place she felt assured it would evade discovery, and went home two hours later with itchy breasts.

Celia focused on filling her spoon with broth and raising it to her mouth without spilling. Her soup was half gone when she felt a tap on her shoulder.

"Hello, Celia."

Becky's eyes were trapped in the face of a middle-aged woman with visible pores and crow's feet, her temples freckled from sun. That Celia recognized the decline of her own face in Becky's grown-up features did nothing to soften the shock of having to swap her childhood Becky for this dilapidated model. The grown-up Becky was dressed more stylishly than the other restaurant clientele, in clothes that might not have seemed prescribed outside the company of so many skirts and shirtsleeves of identical length. Celia couldn't tell whether she was meant to kiss, clasp hands, or merely smile at this person, the question of their lapsed friendship further complicated by possible religious bans. Celia stood.

"Becky!" she said. "Thanks so much for coming!"

When Becky grazed the side of Celia's face with her cheek, her head was close enough to reveal her wig. Celia briefly wondered if, on top of everything else, Becky had cancer, before it occurred to Celia that she was the only woman in the restaurant not wearing one.

"It's not every day an old friend comes to Scranton," Becky demurred. "It was no trouble." She looked at Celia's soup bowl. "I'm sorry, did I keep you waiting?"

"Not at all. I was early."

"Smooth sailing on I-81? I wondered if maybe you were coming from Jensenville."

Celia nodded. "My parents are still there."

"How wonderful! Do you see them often?"

"Not really. It's hard to get away."

When the waiter arrived, Becky ordered for them both. "I imagine this is a cultural experience for you, so I want to be a good guide. Blum's gets their Nova from Zabar's, and Zabar's is the best there is. Have you had lox before?"

"Sure," Celia said. "It's delicious."

"It must be nice," Becky continued, "coming here like this. To Jensenville, I mean. To your childhood home. I haven't been back in I don't know how long." Her eyes lit up. "You haven't been by my old street, have you?"

Celia shook her head.

"I'd love to know if our tree is still there," Becky said. "The one we used to spy from."

Friedrich Street. Becky had lived on Friedrich Street. "It was on the corner!" Celia said. "In front of that old man's house—"

"Mr. Luff," Becky said. "He *hated* us."

Celia bared her teeth. "Get out of my tree!" she growled. "And you would always explain that it wasn't his tree, that the first five feet of lawn actually belonged to the township."

"Public right of way," Becky confirmed.

"How did you *know* that?"

Becky shrugged. "My brain was a sponge back then. I'm not sure right-of-way applied to tree climbing, but I sure did like saying it to Mr. Luff."

"I loved that tree," Celia said. "And your room."

"Oh, Celia, so did I." Becky sighed. "The rainbow wall. My mom painted it. When we moved, I knew I was too old to ask for another one."

Becky's smile was the same strange amalgam it had always been, half happy/half distracted as if her brain, while relaying the command to her mouth, had been called away on more pressing business. An intervening lifetime had not changed Celia's impression that Becky was one of the smartest people she would ever know.

"So," Celia said. "How long have you—" She groped for a word.

"—been religious?" Becky offered.

Celia sipped her water. With her spoon she nudged her matzoh ball to the center of its bowl. "Actually," she stalled, "I was going to ask how long you had been living in Scranton."

"Then you're trying to be polite," Becky replied. "Which is

nice, but unnecessary. After today we won't see each other again, so let's only bother to ask exactly what we want to know."

Celia nodded. It was all coming back—the forthrightness, the showy preference for straight talk. Celia remembered a tour received within minutes of her first visit to Becky's home at some irreclaimable point in third grade, highlighted by Becky's pride in her unmade sheets ("It's my room, I'm the only one who has to see them") and the *Penthouse* magazine Mr. Miller kept under his side of the box frame ("Kind of obvious, isn't it?"). Becky was becoming familiar again, the mantle of middle age displaced by the girl inside.

"I discovered Chabad toward the end of high school," Becky said. "Everyone was talking about college except for me and Leanne—don't look so surprised."

"I'm not," Celia attempted.

"You are," Becky corrected.

"You were such a good student."

"Not by then," Becky said. "By the time Leanne and I were sixteen . . . Let's just say that among our many common interests Leanne had a car, I wanted to get away, and we both liked to sneak off to find college students who would get us high." She shook her head. "Anyway, I was deep into a dedicated career of delinquency when I met a Jewish boy who had been going to the Chabad on campus. I started going there with him and it was the first thing to make sense in a long, long time. That was where I met Shimon—and the rest, as they say, is history." She shrugged. "It's not as crazy as you think. How old were we when we knew each other? Ten? Eleven?"

Celia nodded.

"I was so incredibly anxious back then. The night before a spelling test, I wouldn't be able to sleep. On days I brought home perfect scores, my parents didn't seem to fight as much." She glanced at Celia. "You're so easily shocked. It's probably a good thing you're only seeing me again now that I'm an old-fashioned Jewish housewife." Becky smiled, her face a map of happy lines. "Hey, do you remember the time we decided to be archaeologists and dig for prehistoric bones in your back-yard? We found a piece of a broken plate beneath a bush and decided it was from Colonial times. You said I could have it if I would be your best friend."

Celia nodded. She wasn't sure.

Becky sighed. "I kept that plate for a long, long time."

Celia wanted to ask if the wig itched, if Becky was ever allowed to show off her knees, if she remembered their third-grade teacher saying she could become the country's first female president.

"So," Celia offered. "Your husband's name is Shimon?"

Becky nodded. "He teaches at the yeshiva. Plus he writes poetry. Not as good as yours"—she smiled—"but not bad. Do you still write?"

Celia shrugged. "Not really. I kept it up through college, but then—"

"Oh Celia," Becky chided. "You could have been a con-tender."

Celia laughed. "I was never that serious."

Becky shook her head. "You were! You had us all con-vinced. Mrs. Hogue was always putting your poems on the bulletin board. My desk was right next to that board, and I read them over and over again, but creativity isn't something you can study for. I was sure you were going to be the next Longfellow." She glanced at Celia's hands. "One of several surprises, I suppose. I thought you'd be married."

Celia remembered admiring Becky for using the word *urinate* instead of *tinkle*, for pointing out when their teacher had food stuck between her teeth. Until now, Celia had never considered the origins of her own attraction to directness, Huck's desirability partly based on a seed sown in third grade.

"I have a boyfriend," Celia said. "We live in Chicago. He's a high school teacher—"

"Just like Shimon!"

Celia nodded. "And I work for the city."

"And you come back to Jensenville to visit," Becky said, her eyes far away. "Tell your mother I say hello. She was always so nice to me. Now tell me about Leanne. The last time she and I were in touch she wasn't doing so well. Is she better these days?"

"I don't know," Celia said. "I've just had the one e-mail."

"I choose to take that as a promising sign," Becky said. "I'm not sure I can say we were good *for* each other, but we were certainly good *to* each other. Completely loyal—we'd learned the importance of that." Becky shook her head. "So please tell her that the number she has for me still works. Tell her that she's welcome to call me anytime." The waiter brought a platter layered with slices of dark pink fish. "Okay," Becky continued. "Now tell me why we're here."

For the third time since Becky had arrived, Celia tried not to look surprised.

"Not that I'm not happy to see you," Becky continued. "I didn't have to agree to come, after all. But I am curious. You didn't sound like someone calling on a whim. And you don't actually have business here. This is Scranton, after all. Now tell me, what can I do for you?"

Celia paled. "I'm sorry. It's just, I was afraid if I told you over the phone, I'd scare you away." She looked at the food on her plate, the soup in her bowl, the face of the person she had once sworn to like best of all. "I'd like to talk about what happened," she began.

Becky nodded. "I used to wonder if it haunted you." Her eyes searched Celia's face. "Do you know I actually wrote a speech? An eloquent denunciation and exculpation I planned to deliver when you asked to be my friend again. I made a minor career out of avoiding you in middle school, waiting for you to seek me out and plead for my forgiveness. But you never did."

"I managed to block it out for a long, long time," Celia said.

"Really?" Becky said. "That's a neat trick. I'm still ashamed by our cruelty, and that's after having apologized to Leanne twenty years ago!"

Two women gazed at each other from across a chasm, each waiting for the other to recognize what lay on the other side.

"I'm sorry," Celia said, "but I'm not sure I know what you mean."

Becky looked at Celia, her mouth hanging open. "I mean all the ways you and Djuna tortured that poor girl! The daily ratings, the dress code." She shook her head. "When Leanne and I were first becoming friends, *real* friends, you were one of the main things we talked about. For what it's worth, I defended you. I told Leanne you were different before Djuna came along, that Djuna was a bad influence. Of course, you weren't the only one at fault. Josie and I let it happen. We never tried to stop you."

Celia remembered giggling in the bathroom; she remembered notes passed between desks. She had a vague sense of something, a familiar strain from a forgotten tune.

"I thought I was protecting myself," Becky continued. "I was afraid that if I tried to defend Leanne, I would be next. The day I knew I had to say something, the day you really took things too far, it was over. And do you know that part of me was secretly glad? I thought it served her right, getting into that car. A terrible thing to think, I know. When I look at Chaya, my oldest, and realize how young we all were—no one deserves what happened to Djuna . . . not even Djuna."

For a moment, neither spoke.

"What do you remember about that day?" Celia began.

"No," Becky countered. "You tell me what *you* remember. After all these years of wondering, I think I deserve to know. You saw more than any of us except Djuna herself, and I have a feeling she won't be looking me up."

At a table across the room, two younger versions of Becky—both pregnant, both with children impatient to be fed—dealt out bagels with the sangfroid of blackjack dealers. The older children passed out napkins, their faces mirroring the mothers' bored efficiency.

Celia closed her eyes and took a breath.

"I remember it was a pretty day," she began. "The kind where it was hard to focus on anything except being outside. When the five of us started walking—"

"I was so terrified," Becky said. "I mean, we were *not* supposed to be there. It was like a highway, that road. No sidewalks. All those cars. Going there was the sort of thing a bad kid did. And at that point I was not a bad kid."

"Djuna and I were ahead of the rest of you," Celia continued. "We were arguing about I don't know what, and right when we were about to round a curve, Djuna ran ahead—"

"You were fighting about Leanne," Becky interrupted. "I'd never seen Djuna angrier, which, given your fights, is saying a lot. We were at one of the bigger curves in the road, though there wasn't any railing anywhere . . . just the road, then gravel, and then trees. You told the rest of us to wait while you went after her, and you had us so well trained that for a while we actually did it."

"Djuna went into the woods after we came around the curve," Celia said. "I followed her in, but before I could get to her, she fell. I watched it happen, and when Djuna didn't get right back up, I went back out the way we'd come. I just left her there."

Becky had a look on her face that Celia couldn't read.

"Becky," Celia said. "I lied to you that day. I told you that Djuna got into a car, but she didn't. She never came out of those woods."

Becky exhaled a long, tired breath, the fraternal twin of the sound Celia had heard over the phone. Celia realized that smoking was the habit Becky indulged when she was alone.

"I wish I could be more specific," Celia continued, "but I can't. All I know is that she must have fallen into a hole of some sort. Because of the way it happened. She was there one moment, and then the next, she was gone and I didn't—"

"Celia."

Celia felt as if she'd been yanked from a dream.

"You remember my father?" Becky asked. She studied Celia from across the table. "Stupid question. Of course you remember him. Well, somehow, he doesn't seem to remember ever hitting my mother."

Celia gestured as if to push Becky's words away with her hands.

"I know!" Becky exclaimed. "Can you believe it? About five years ago, I talked to him. First time since I was thirteen. What he remembers is the time he picked up a lamp and threw it against the wall. Heirloom lamp. Belonged to my mother's grandmother. He feels terrible about it. The wrong way to end a marriage that had to end some way, he told me." Becky smiled. "I didn't try to correct him. No point. Plus, he didn't ask for my opinion. But in this instance you *have* asked, so I'll tell you this: I remember standing by the side of the road while you and Djuna went off to argue. Leanne wasn't wearing a single one of the right colors. Before, she'd always tried to have something—lavender socks, a pink belt. But that day, it was like she had been deliberately trying to take things too far. You haven't mentioned the haircut, but that's fine with me; it makes me sick to think of it. Let's skip ahead. Until that afternoon, at least when it came to Leanne, you and Djuna had always been a united front. You having second thoughts when we got to the road . . . well, it really pissed Djuna off. You and she had just gone around the curve. Leanne was with me and Josie, staring in your direction with this almost hungry look." Becky shook her head. "That was when I decided to say something. And when I was spared from having to."

Becky stared at Celia as if she had forgotten where she was. "If I had come around that curve just a little earlier I would have seen Djuna getting in. That would have been harder to live with, I think, because I might have been stuck thinking I could have done something about it. As it was, the car was already pulling away. When the policeman asked me, all I could tell him was 'brown.' You told us she'd gotten a ride home. You said that we had to go straight to her house to make sure. I wasn't sure why, but you said it with such certainty that I didn't bother to argue. I spent that walk thinking it was a new beginning, that you and I could finally be friends like before. I was so impressed that you'd stood up to her, that we'd both reached a breaking point at the same time. When we got to Djuna's, I was going to invite you back to my house, right in front of her. Then we arrived, and Mrs. Pearson answered the door, and of course Djuna wasn't there. That was when you said you hadn't recognized the driver and I understood why we'd made the walk. It was the word *stranger* that did it. Use that word with *car* and it only means one thing. The mind is good at selective forgetting—Yoshi, the baby, isn't six months yet and already his birth is fuzzy in my mind—but I still remember standing on

Djuna's front walk, not even knowing I'd peed my pants until I felt it against my leg. Even now, when I think back to you on that road, I'm still impressed. If it had been me, I think I would have gone too. Knowing it was a terrible idea, I would have gotten in that car because Djuna already had. I've always wondered how you managed not to do it. I've wondered about that more than I care to admit."

"Becky," Celia said. "There was no car."

She had meant to say it quietly, but the women at a neighboring table turned to look. Becky smiled and said something in a language Celia didn't understand. The women laughed. Becky's gaze canvassed the dining room before her mouth relaxed again. When she looked at Celia, her eyes were soft.

"Listen, Celia," she said. "Because I have a simple answer for you." Becky leaned toward her, and in the angle of Becky's neck Celia glimpsed a girl seeking artifacts in upturned soil. "Tell Leanne that you're sorry. An apology is a powerful thing. It's the advice I would have given my father, if he had ever asked."

Becky gazed at her watch, then stood and offered her hand. When Celia rose too, Becky cupped Celia's face and kissed her on both cheeks. "*Zei gezunt*, Celia. Be well." By the time Celia noticed the money for the bill, it was too late to give any of it back.

Driving home, Celia owed her safe return to a straight road and few cars, to sixty miles of highway that accommodated a full brain. Becky's words had knocked something loose, something oddly shaped with a jagged edge. Celia wasn't sure how the daily ratings had started, only that Leanne had presented herself for inspection each morning. Sometimes she tied her stringy hair into a limp ponytail; sometimes she switched her worn cords for a faded dress. Once, Leanne had proudly presented nails a shade of red filched from her mother's drawer, the polish overreaching each ragged nail onto the cuticle and fingertip. Negative points, they had told her, too messy a job. Then there was the time Celia and Djuna had surprised Leanne in the girls' bathroom. With a little boost, Djuna had been able to peer over the stall door at Leanne with her panties around her ankles. Leanne had shrieked as if she'd been smacked. "Just checking," Djuna had said before she and Celia had run, giggling, into the hall.

When Celia returned to Schubert Street the phone was ringing. She dashed to pick it up, certain it was Mrs. Linke, terrified that if she didn't answer she wouldn't get another chance.

"Hello?" she panted.

"Cee?"

Jeremy had a late-night radio DJ's voice that, at its onset, had sounded like a practical joke, puberty's first shuffle-step having created a puny, smooth-cheeked boy who sounded like Isaac Hayes. The initial shock of that odd timing had never worn off. Even now Jeremy spoke quietly, still apologizing for a discrepancy long since corrected.

"What's wrong?" Celia asked, her pulse racing. The last time her brother had called was to announce that Daniel had been born, and before that Celia couldn't remember. Holiday visits had always been enough, their parents filling in the gaps between.

"Nothing," he said, and Celia realized that it was true. This was not her phone, not her house, not a place where her idea of normal applied. "But are you okay?" he asked. "You sound a little strange."

"Sorry. I forgot where I was. When the phone rang, I just—"

"No worries," he said. "I was just calling about Saturday. Mom wasn't sure whether you wanted to do brunch or dinner, and I was going to leave a message to say that either would be fine." He paused. "You know, I was kind of surprised when Mom said you were here."

"It was pretty spontaneous," Celia said.

"Is something up? You're not sick or anything, are you? Or are you and Huck—"

"We're fine. I'm fine." Celia walked to the kitchen's edge and then back again, a reflex from a corded age. "I'm trying to track down some old friends. I'll tell you about it when you come on Saturday."

"Who?"

"Huh?"

"Who are you trying to track down?"

When awareness of her cordless state erased the desire to pace, Celia sank into a kitchen chair. "You probably wouldn't remember her, but I actually just came back from seeing Becky Miller."

"Becky Miller," Jeremy echoed. "Brainy girl with bangs and bony arms. Crazy-sounding laugh. You and her were always going off on expeditions."

"Jem, how do you know that? You were, like, seven at the time." Her father's chair offered a wider backyard view than her own place at the table. Celia could see all the way to the side-yard privacy fence, its cedar planking a bulwark against a rising tide.

"Pam calls it my elephant brain," Jeremy said. "But Becky's easy. She saved my life."

"What?"

"Well, not really, but it felt like it at the time. The three of us were coming back from the creek."

"I forgot you would play with us," Celia said. "She really liked having you around."

"I think I was the closest she ever got to being an older sister," Jeremy said. "Anyway, we were crossing a street on the way home, when I stepped into a place in the road where the asphalt had fallen in. It wasn't big enough for a traffic cone. I don't think it was much bigger than a kid's foot, but I managed to step in it anyway and went down past my knee. A car was coming, but I was so surprised that I didn't move. You and Becky were already across. You were yelling at me to get out of the street, but Becky ran back out and held up her hand to stop the car. You felt bad because you were supposed to have been holding my hand. Even if the car hadn't seen me it would have missed me. It was a pretty wide road, but when Becky did that she became a superhero, or at least someone I knew I was going to marry someday. It's funny, hearing her name again."

Celia tried to call up Jeremy's story but could only summon its constituent parts, a handful of jigsaw pieces that seemed drawn from different puzzles.

"Jem," she asked into the phone, "was I ever cruel?"

"It wasn't like you left me in the road on purpose. It was an accident."

"I don't mean then," Celia said. "I mean in general. Was I?"

Jeremy laughed. "What would make you think that?"

"But if I was, you would tell me, right?" she asked.

"Sure, but you weren't. You were a pretty good big sister. If you want mean, you should talk to Pam; her brothers make the rest of us look like saints."

Celia tried to assess her reflection in the kitchen window. She felt unequal to memory's hidden mechanism of cogs and wheels.

"Seeing Becky today made me think about someone else I used to know, a girl named Leanne."

She waited.

"Her I don't remember," Jeremy said. "You must not have brought her home. Look, how are the dogs? Are the dogs all right?"

Her brother had only ever seen pictures. "The dogs are good."

"Good," said Jeremy. "I'll see you Saturday, then. Brunch, dinner, whatever. And if you don't mind me asking, where is Becky?"

"Becky?"

"You said you saw her?"

"She lives in Scranton, if you can believe it."

"Wow, Scranton." He paused. "Is she happy?"

Celia hadn't considered it. "Yeah," she told him. "I think she is."

"Happy is good," Jeremy said.

CHAPTER 9

Returning to her brother's room after hanging up with him felt like trespassing, but Celia had nowhere else to go. To postpone coming back to the computer, she briefly pivoted right instead of left at the end of the hall. Stripped of meaningful possessions, her old bedroom had succumbed to that universal law regarding nature and vacuums: the closet had been overrun by her parents' off-season clothes, and gifts from two careers of office holiday parties populated the bottom drawers of her old bureau. The room's edges had been colonized by assorted boxes—financial documents, wrapping paper, Christmas decorations—all easier to fetch from an unoccupied bedroom than from beneath the attic's low-hung ceiling. The few remaining childhood items—the high bed with its dotted quilt and matching bed skirt, a faded poster of Elton John, the shelf that held a dusty souvenir glass from junior prom, an abandoned *Child's Garden of Verses*, and several nondescript stuffed animals that had failed to inspire names—were too scant to project a younger self among them. Celia felt no more attached to this room than a hermit crab to its discarded shell.

The same feeling had found her earlier that week in Chicago, though thinking back to Monday felt like peering into a funhouse mirror that stretched three days into something impossibly distant. The street corner had grown blurry in her mind, and all that remained of the office were Gary's and Helene's expressions, but Celia remembered the reverse commute, the girls' giddy barks at the sound of her arrival, the click of their nails on the far side of the apartment door, and finally the reprieve of Bella and Sylvie licking her face, their bodies solid and warm and forgiving everything. Celia had been sitting on the couch when the apartment became a museum. She had pictured a placard beside Huck's guitar in its corner, curatorial labels beside the photos she'd had matted and framed to celebrate their first year in the apartment, even an instructive diagram of herself sitting on her customary couch cushion on the left-hand side, Huck to her right. In the time between that morning's departure and her return, these had become historical truths, artifacts from her life as it had once been.

Huck liked to point out that history was a retrospective pastime. Because it was impossible to intuit the future significance of any given moment, it was always a good idea to be your best possible self, increasing the odds of not wanting to disown whatever inadvertent history you created. What was Huck's rallying cry in the classroom became his mantra when he got particularly stoned at parties and propounded upon the potential future significance of this *very* moment, this one *right now*. The idea charmed or irritated Celia, depending on her mood, but sitting with the dogs on the couch that Monday she had sensed its truth. Earlier that morning—as she and Huck had gotten dressed, toasted their bagels, and headed out into their respective days—they had unwittingly experienced the end of an era, the last link of a deteriorating chain.

Inside the evacuation zone of Jeremy's old room, Celia sat at her brother's desk. Its surface had once hosted an evolving array of fantasy figurines, game cartridges, baseball books, and CDs. Now there was just her father's computer, a Conklin Junior College mug with pens and a pair of scissors, and a Mensa calendar abandoned at a puzzle for a Wednesday three Aprils past. On a faded Post-it note attached to the monitor, a list in Warren's hand proposed *Furnace?, Chimney?, Tax Receipts, Vacuum Cleaner Bags*, with only the last two items crossed through. Beyond the desk, Jeremy's bare mattress had been draped with a green blanket that still bore creases from its original packaging. Its crispness, like that of the new carpet, was at odds with the empty shelves, the patched walls, the flaccid curtains sewn from bedsheets so long ago that the sun had bleached their blue stripes to gray.

Leanne had already written back. The e-mail's electronic postmark awakened in Celia a dormant species of hive knowledge: Leanne had pressed Send while Celia and Becky had been conducting their mutual interview. Once upon a time,

Celia had known when Djuna ate her dinner, when Becky took her bath. She had prized this information with the inarticulate ardor that presages sex. Back when passion was still in utero—a beating heart without legs—its rudiments had been present but primal, means that had not yet acquired perceivable ends. Friendship had been fathomed by phone—*It's four thirty, are you watching* The Flintstones?—the question both test and assertion. Djuna was always right, even when she wasn't—but when Becky or Josie called, Celia would sometimes deny them. *No, I'm doing homework*, she would say, muting the television to make it seem true. As Celia stared at Leanne's name on the computer screen, she wondered what Josie had been doing at 1:43 P.M., the diminished hydra of their friendship briefly revived.

> **From:** Lee Forrest
> **To:** Celia Durst
> **Subject:** Re: Re:
>
> Celia—You wanted to know if I still think about
> Djuna. The past isn't something I spend a whole lot
> of time on anymore, but sometimes I wonder about
> the guy who took her. Mostly if he wants to find
> forgiveness or if he even knows what he did. If he
> was tricked up on something, he might have been a
> stranger even to himself. It's a miracle my own
> memory didn't go the way of my liver, though a
> little amnesia might have been nice. At least when it
> came time for me to make my amends, writing out

my list was pretty straightforward. By the way, I told my sponsor about that people-finding Web site. I wish that sort of thing had been around seven years ago.

Since you said you wanted to face up to what happened when we were kids, I'm guessing that you're trying to make some amends of your own. It's true you weren't the nicest person to me back then and sometimes you were just plain evil, but it's not like I put up a fight. If you were even half as miserable as I was, it's a wonder you didn't act five times worse, which is my way of saying that if you've got your own list you're working your way down, you can consider me crossed off. I didn't hold on to any of that stuff after Djuna disappeared. To be honest, I think I saw what happened to her as a sort of rough justice. Just goes to show what a vindictive little fucker I was when I was a girl.

If you do end up tracking Becky down, let me know how she's doing, okay?

—Lee

Once Celia reached the end of the message, she scrolled back to the top and read it again, to amend the nervous rush of her first read. Late afternoon light through the window cast her profile on the near wall. Noreen and Warren's bedroom displayed a framed silhouette of a younger Celia cut from black construction paper. Its nose was an indistinct nub, but its lips and chin were miniature versions of Celia's adult shadow.

She thought to consult her watch only after she had dialed.

"Can I call you back?" Huck asked. "I'm with a student."

Celia tried to say something that passed for acquiescence.

"You sound terrible," he said. "Hang on."

His voice disappeared, then returned.

"You still there?"

"I'm sorry," she said. "I didn't check the time."

"It's all right. School's out. Jackson was just hanging around. Tell me what's going on."

"Wait," she said. She left her brother's room and crossed the hall. She closed the bedroom door behind her, habit guarding her conversation from the hollow ear of the empty house.

"I found them," she said.

The bed beneath her dotted quilt held her like a steadying palm. Celia started with Josie, then proceeded to Becky in Scranton. "I was prepared for Becky to be surprised," she said, "but not for her to believe that she had actually *seen* the car."

The silence that followed was just long enough to cause Celia's jaw to clench.

"What exactly did Becky say about it?" Huck asked. "I mean, did she basically repeat the same story you told back then or did she—"

"She said that she remembered seeing a brown car. I didn't ask her for details, okay? I mean, why would I ask about something that didn't exist?"

When Celia closed her eyes, she saw Becky leaning across

the table, her face close enough to show the bobby pins along the edge of her scalp.

"The whole time I was in that restaurant," Celia said, "I kept thinking about the dress-up drawer that Becky had in third grade. She and I would put on her mother's old clothes and invent stories about ourselves. Part of me kept expecting Becky to take off her wig and tell me that she didn't have seven kids after all."

Celia sat on the edge of the bed, surprised by how easily her feet reached the floor. She could remember her toes dangling at the level of the box spring, the carpet reached only after a moment's free fall.

"Jem called," she said.

"Did you tell him?"

"Not really."

"Why not?" Huck was convinced of the redemptive powers of sibling communication, a faith consecrated inside the silent cathedral of the only child.

"It wasn't a conversation I wanted to have on the phone," Celia said. "He's coming on Saturday with Pam and Daniel. Oh, and I forgot to tell you: Pam's pregnant."

Celia heard something in Huck contract.

"Daddy called it a happy accident," she said.

Perhaps brothers or sisters on Huck's side would have provided a broader spectrum of married and unmarried, begetting and abstaining, into which they might have more comfortably fit. Instead, the birth notices of friends or colleagues went undisplayed on fridge and table, weren't even kept inside a bureau drawer. The silent interval that followed now was just long enough for Huck to tuck Celia's news away like one of those 5x7 envelopes whose stiffness betrayed the presence of the photo inside.

"Talk to me about Becky," he said. "What was it like?"

"It's always weird to see someone again after so long," she said. "But the hard part was when Becky reminded me how mean we had been."

Celia suspected she had elided her part in Leanne's humiliation less from shame than because it had not seemed wrong at the time. To Celia at age eleven, their collective behavior had felt natural, Leanne the rodent to their parliament of owls. The reeducation of a tomboy had been a harmless prank, uncritically shelved. But it was true: they had been mean. There was always a window of opportunity in the morning, between when the buses arrived and when Mrs. Grandy led them into the school. Standing Leanne against the flagpole had lent their scrutiny an official air. Starting from her head, they worked their way down, inspecting the way she pushed her hair behind her ears, the slope of her neck as it emerged from her shirt, or some other random aspect of Leanne's body completely beyond her control. Occasionally they gave Leanne homework, and she would show up the next day wearing something with flowers on it, or having curled her bangs. A passed inspection meant she was free to join them at lunch and recess; failure meant she had to earn their company. Leanne's willingness to forgive Celia and even tender a motive for her cruelty had induced the shame Celia should have been feeling all along. Her behavior had no excuse. Celia had not been the half-miserable girl of Leanne's creation. She had abused Leanne simply because she could.

"It's just so hard for me to picture all this," Huck said.

"Why?"

"Because I know you!"

"People change," Celia said. "I have a hard time believing some of the stories from when you were sixteen."

"Yeah," said Huck, "but a sixteen-year-old boy and an eleven-year-old girl are completely different animals."

Celia wondered how she had managed half a lifetime of sleep on such a hard bed.

"Ceel," Huck said. "Try to be kind to yourself. You're doing everything you can."

"But what if everyone is like Mommy and Becky?" she said. "What if no one believes me?"

She sensed what was coming next, began shaking her head even before Huck could ask.

"Well, do you think there's any chance that Becky might be right?"

Celia held her breath.

"Just hear me out," Huck said. "I'm not suggesting that Becky *is* right, or your mother. All I'm asking is that if someone's memory is wrong, is there a possibility that it could be yours?"

She exhaled.

"You don't have to do this," she said.

"Do what?"

"Find a way to absolve me."

"I'm not trying to find anything," Huck said, "I'm only wondering if—"

"There's nothing to wonder about, Huck." Celia closed her eyes and watched Djuna fall in slow motion. "I *know* what I did. And it explains so many things."

"Ceel, there's nothing to—"

"Just stop, Huck. Of course there is. Everyone knows it's not *you*. For years you've been patient, biding your time with your students and the girls."

"Come on, Ceel," Huck said. "Bella and Sylvie were your idea!"

"Of course they were!" she hissed. "But without them I think you would have left me a long time ago."

Celia was shivering, her body shaking in a way that had nothing to do with cold. She stood from the bed as if to retrieve her words. The silence at the other end of the line was the pause between dropping a stone and waiting for it to hit bottom.

"You know," Huck said, "until you left on Monday, I had no idea how depressed I'd become."

Celia pulled her quilt from the bed and wrapped it around herself, the fabric stiff with age. "It's been like watching a car crash in slow motion," she said. "It's been like this slow, steady bleed."

"Don't cry," Huck said. "The last thing I want to do is make you cry."

Their stillness amplified the distance, sadness that stretched for hundreds of miles.

"Ceel?"

She pinched the bridge of her nose, feeling the tension there gather and disperse.

"Call me tonight when your folks are asleep," he continued. "Call me and we won't talk about any of this."

"Why?"

"Because right now I have to make sure that Jackson isn't wandering the halls tagging lockers, and then I have to drive home before Bella and Sylvie start peeing in the kitchen. We shouldn't have started this conversation . . . not like this, over the phone . . . but now that we have, I don't want it to be what I'm thinking about when I go to sleep."

"Don't go yet," she said.

"I love you, Ceel."

"Promise?" She felt like she was five years old.

"Promise," he said, and she told herself that she felt better.

CHAPTER 10

At dinner, Celia reminded herself that the table's empty chair was a temporary vacancy, but this did not banish her sense that some sort of non-elective surgery had been performed. The first time she'd brought Huck home, her parents had been so excited to have more than a name over the phone that he could have been a chain-smoker, a man twice her age, or a long-haul trucker and they would have treated him like nobility. Instead he was an aspiring history teacher who laughed at Warren's jokes, and they had treated him like a son. Even so, it had taken two more Christmases before Noreen stopped asking Celia about her Chicago life and started asking, "How is Huck?" Celia had inherited her mother's sense of caution. During

Huck's first visit, Celia had been alternately gabby and silent, tense and at ease, until finally on the last night she had burst into tears while they lay together in bed. "You're still here!" she'd confessed into the warmth of his neck, knowing how ridiculous it sounded and how deep her relief that it was true. Tonight, Warren had turned himself up a notch in compensation for Huck's absence, his voice striving to fill the void. Noreen had set pitchers of water and iced tea on the table to disguise the place where Huck's plate should have been.

"Did the two of you talk today?" she asked, as if the mention of Huck's name might spoil her careful beverage arrangement along the table's empty side.

"We did," Celia said. "He sends his love."

Since the previous morning, mother and daughter had been treating each other like circumstantial seatmates on a long-distance bus ride. It had been years since they had stooped to such depths of courtesy at such close range, not since the protracted sigh that had lasted the four months between Celia's decision to forgo Cornell and the commencement of her Midwestern migration.

"Is he still coming?" Warren said.

"Warren!" Noreen winced.

Celia squelched the urge to run from the table, mount the stairs, and slam her bedroom door. "Why would you even ask that, Daddy?"

"No reason, I suppose." He shrugged. "It's just that I know how busy a teacher can get, and you do look a little down-at-the-mouth. I guess I was just wondering if the two of you—"

"This isn't about me and Huck, okay?" Celia had mastered an older version of this exchange, complete with hair flips and narrowed eyes. Holding it back felt like strangling a sneeze. "I mean, sure, he's worried, and he's got a lot of the same . . . concerns as you and Mommy do. So I'm trying to help him put some of those to rest, but it's hard. I mean, everything I'm trying to do . . . with you, and with Huck, and with people I don't even *know* anymore . . . so if I seem a little *down-at-the-mouth* . . ." She took a shaky breath.

"We used to worry," Noreen said. "In high school, and then for most of college, you never mentioned anybody special. I used to think to myself, 'What if my little girl never finds her true love?' " Noreen smiled. "Some people say there are all sorts of people who are right for each other and it's a matter of any one of them being in the right place at the right time, but I just don't believe that. The minute I met your father, I knew he was the one."

"So if there's anything we can do to help . . ." Warren gestured at the empty air. "With Huck, or with anything else . . ."

Celia stared at her father until he turned away. It didn't take long.

"For example, if you wanted us to talk to him," he offered to his water glass. "To give him our perspective on this whole thing."

"Look, Daddy, there's nothing you could tell Huck that he doesn't know already. Can we . . . Can you . . . How about we talk about something else?"

Cutting and chewing took over. Warren ate like a man

possessed, while Noreen divided her meal into fork-friendly pieces. Celia shuttled the food into her mouth and made the requisite jaw motions without tasting a thing.

"Jem told me that you and he got a chance to chat," Noreen said.

"When?" Celia asked.

"Oh, we speak almost every day." It was hard not to admire the precision of her mother's movements, an entire dinner reduced to one-inch squares. "Sometimes he'll call from work, other times he'll call in the evening. It's funny, but when I look at what happened to him and what has come of it . . ." She shook her head. "When you said yesterday that I didn't know him . . ." Noreen looked between her silverware and her plate of portioned food. There was nothing more to cut.

"I didn't mean that," Celia said.

"No, no," Noreen said. "It's true. I *didn't* know him back then. I loved him, of course, and I worried for him, and I tried to give him what I thought he needed, but to really know a person, especially your own child . . . A sense of independence is so important, not to mention a sense of trust, and if you want to give your child those, well, I think that *knowing* them is a sacrifice you might have to make."

"It worked with you," Warren said. "Look at you now: independent, a successful career . . . though I have to say it was hard letting you go."

Noreen nodded. "Jem missed you terribly when you left," she said. "In a way, I think it was harder on him. All his life he'd had a sister, and then you were gone."

Celia's absence from what had easily been her family's most traumatic period often left her feeling like she had slept through some crucial historic event—the siege of Leningrad, for example, or the Great Depression. Not for the first time, she pondered what might have been had she attended a school fifty rather than seven hundred miles away.

"He never told me," Celia said.

"No point," Warren said.

"You'd made your decision," Noreen said, "and fourteen-year-old boys aren't exactly known for sharing their feelings."

Celia felt as if she were attending a class reunion with people she had only passed in the halls.

"Then I guess you know that Becky Miller lives in Scranton," she said.

"Jem mentioned it," Noreen confirmed. "That must have been a surprise."

"Which one was Becky?" Warren asked.

"The sad, pale one who spoke in complex sentences," her mother explained.

"The one who could recite the state capitals in alphabetical order?"

"That was her."

Celia's father cocked his head. "She was the one who didn't think I was funny."

"You two played so nicely together," Noreen said. "And Becky was so full of ideas! She was smart, that one. Scranton would not have been my first guess."

"We met at a kosher deli," Celia said. "She's Hasidic now."

"Really?" Noreen asked. "You know, sometimes when she

was over, I'd watch from the kitchen window as the two of you played in the backyard. Not to keep an eye on you. The way you got along, I didn't have to. You were like sisters, the way you played. I used to think . . ." She smiled. "It's silly, but it's what you do with your children. I pictured Becky as the friend you might grow up with, the one who'd always be around. Who would have thought . . ." She shook her head. "Were you able to recognize her? After all those years?"

"Her eyes hadn't changed," Celia said.

Warren pointed to his daughter's face. "The eyeball is the only part of the body that starts out practically full-grown."

The meal was one of Celia's favorites, its name having long ago been changed in her honor to Chicken à la Queen. Once she had learned from Huck that cooked vegetables could be crunchy and that meat didn't have to be the same color all the way through, she had felt briefly obliged to consider her mother a lousy cook. This reluctant verdict—imposed by culinary self-consciousness and the discovery of haricots verts— was soon overruled by her long-standing love for string bean casserole with canned onion bits. Neither fusion cuisine nor New American could cheapen Celia's love for her mother's cooking, or sully the appeal of a table consecrated to the provincial Mid-Atlantic palate. She wondered if this particular meal was meant as a peace offering or as a spur to her guilt, but decided it was just as likely what they were meant to have eaten yesterday, the chicken poached ahead of time and then made to languish an extra day in the refrigerator, pining for sauce and toast.

"Did you and Becky have a lot to talk about?" her mother asked.

"Sure they did," her father said. "It's always nice to see an old friend."

Celia was seduced by the simplicity of her relationship to her meal. It was too much food, really, a plate filled according to a mother's concern and not a daughter's appetite.

"How could you tell back then that Becky was sad?" Celia asked.

Noreen sighed. "You wouldn't have recognized it, thank goodness. For you, sadness at that age meant missing a birthday party or not getting dessert, but Becky laughed like she knew it was temporary. She reminded me of those paintings—the ones of those children with the big, soulful eyes. You know, the more I think about it, the more it makes a sort of sense, where Becky is now. She always struck me as someone who wanted something different from what she had."

They nodded at the same time. For a moment Celia felt as if she were gazing into a mirror. She recognized her shyness in her mother's smile, the little lines that radiated like ripples from the corners of her upturned mouth. Celia realized why her mother's eyes had always seemed small in photos: Noreen opened them wider for her than for any camera. Celia marveled at how long she had squandered such grace by being unprepared to receive it.

CHAPTER 11

"It's you," Huck said. "What time is it there? Ten?"

"I've been downstairs," she said. "Waiting until I couldn't hear creaking floorboards or water through the pipes. I've been flipping through the channels and pretending you were here." By the time she'd climbed the stairs, her parents' bedroom was dark, their door ajar. Closing herself inside the guest room, she'd rattled the knob to check the latch, the best she could do in the absence of a button to press or a key to turn.

"What did I want to watch?" Huck asked.

"A historical something-or-other about Crispus Attucks," she said. "I only agreed because he's one of your favorites."

"I'm sorry about before," he said. "I was thinking out loud.

I should have saved the subject for when we were in the same time zone."

Celia pressed the phone to her ear.

"Ceel?" he asked. "You still there?"

Through the receiver she heard footsteps, their tone changing as Huck left the living room.

"It's going to be all right," he said.

"I don't know, Huck." Her eyes were closed, her face buried in her hand.

"Let me demonstrate," he said.

"I think I just want to go to bed."

"Me too. I miss you, Ceel. Yesterday when you left, I realized that I've been missing you for a long, long time."

She heard him exhale a shaky breath.

"I go away sometimes," he said, "and it's like I'm looking at everything through backward binoculars. When you kissed me on your way out the door on Tuesday morning, I realized I couldn't remember the last time we had kissed in a way that wasn't good night or good-bye. I've been thinking about that for three days now, and waiting for a chance to make up for it."

Whether it was some slight alteration in the room sound over the phone or just one among the multitude of wordless certainties that their years together had built, the silence between them changed. Celia willed herself toward the shift.

"I miss you too," she said.

"You're in the bedroom?" he said.

"Yeah."

"The door's closed?"

"Of course," she said, checking again to make sure.

"Walk to the mirror."

"I don't know, Huck."

"Let's do this, Ceel. At least let's try."

It was the idea that she might do something for him.

"What are you wearing?" he asked.

"Nothing good," she said. "My green sweater with the black pants. It's what I wore to lunch."

"Your green V-neck?"

"Yeah."

"The one you wear with the camisole?"

"Yeah. Look, tomorrow night, once you're here—"

"No, no," he said. "This is perfect. Now listen: take off your bra and your camisole—but keep the sweater on—and then tell me what you see."

They'd only ever done this once before, years ago. Huck had been attending a teaching conference in Wisconsin. He had woken her with his call, talking low and urgent into the phone. His voice had tipped something inside her.

Celia withdrew her arms from their sleeves and shimmied each in turn down the camisole's inside seam. She remembered her single-minded optimism as she had dressed that morning, then pushed the memory aside. She reached behind to unclasp and slipped her bra straps from her shoulders. She pulled the bra from the bottom, the camisole through the neck. She pictured Huck with the phone pressed to his ear, alive to each slight sound.

"Okay," she said.

"Tell me."

"I took them off just like you said."

"Tell me. You slid your arms out—"

"I took my arms out my sleeves and then took off the camisole from inside the sweater. Then I undid my bra."

"One hand or two?"

"One. I just reached around and—"

"That's right, you just reached around. Now, I know you're standing at the mirror, because I told you to, but I bet you're too far away. Stand close. Stand so that you fill it up."

She moved closer, stood so that her shoulders spanned the mirror's width.

"Okay," she said.

"Can you see your mole?"

"What mole?"

"Have we never talked about this?"

She was unaccustomed to the sweater's weft on her shoulder blades, her nipples.

"I don't think so," she said.

"The red mole on the curve of your left breast. Perched above your cleavage like it's thinking of jumping in. Perfectly round, size of a sugar bead."

She stepped even closer, leaned her head in.

"Oh," she said.

"I bet you can just see it along the left edge of the V-neck."

"How do you know that?"

"It's my job to know. Now listen: I want you to keep that sweater on."

"Okay."

"I want you to keep it on the whole time. And don't think you can fool me. I'll know if you cheat."

"Yes," she said, warmth spreading from the center of her chest.

"Now go back to the bed," he said. "Shuck your pants and panties. I want you naked from the waist down, on your back, knees bent, your legs spread wide."

She tested the guest room door one last time, and wedged a blanket in the space below the door's bottom edge. Then she lay down on the bed and did exactly what Huck told her to do.

CHAPTER 12

She was in the woods, the road in the distance, the silence around her punctuated by the *phwa* of passing cars. She turned her girl's body back around, away from the road, and started back through the trees. She crossed the woods, the road behind her, the branches black slashes against the sky. Celia arrived at a dark hole in the ground the size of a soup bowl and startled awake, fear and longing pounding at her chest. A friendship like hers and Djuna's could only ever be a child's possession. Only a child could withstand its stranglehold.

Celia was dressed and backing the car out of the driveway before she realized she pictured Ripley Road only through school bus windows. The bus windshield view had delivered a seam of pitted asphalt lined by trees, no dashed yellow line to marshal the cars that careened down the hill. One window seat had offered successive slivers of house, glimpsed between trees like a giant zoëtrope. Opposite was a forest from Brothers Grimm, the foliage thick and unruly, and wrapped with vines. These images were unallied to any larger, internal map. Ripley Road had been etched into her memory when destinations were still passive affairs. To get there now, Celia would have to ghost her elementary school bus route, abdicating street names for childhood landmarks: a certain house, a certain street corner, an intersection at an acute angle, a gradual uphill grade past a church and then a quick left-hand turn.

Celia drove on instinct, relying on her child's memory to tell her when to turn. The bus had traced a fractal path through hills, to houses strung like beads along winding back roads. Along the way, Celia encountered a wider road, an expanded church building, a grocery store where once there had been an empty lot, but most of the scenery remained. When she passed the railroad tracks, the plant nursery, the rough-hewn fence that enclosed a tiny clapboard house whose shutters were as green as her memory's claim, each rediscovered landmark resonated within her like a gently plucked string.

The five of them had walked along the road's narrow shoulder. Cars had passed in blasts of speed that launched pebbles at their legs with slingshot force. Celia remembered a pocked speed-limit sign at the curve in the road where Djuna ran ahead. When Celia had started into the woods, the sound of her breath had been drowned out by the percussion of so much tinder underfoot.

There had once been a fire, kindled by lightning, more than a school bus rumor because it had made the local news. This was in second grade, before Djuna's time, when getting a window seat had been the most important thing. The day after the blaze, Celia remembered cupping her hands to her eyes and pressing her face to the rattling window glass. She had pictured trees reduced to charred skeletons, the forest's secrets finally revealed, but the view along the road had remained unchanged. The fire became another story, one more secret the woods kept to itself.

Celia's memory proved a perfect navigator until the final turn. The last street before Ripley felt longer than it should. At the top of the hill, where Celia was expecting an abutment, there was instead a curve that brought her to an unfamiliar traffic signal. She retraced her path in search of a missed turn, but everything until that final intersection matched. She reversed herself once more, driving back toward the unfamiliar traffic light.

When Celia turned through the intersection onto the strange street, she noticed the sign. The narrow, winding road had become a four-lane highway. North- and southbound straightaways extended as far as she could see, a simple exercise in one-point perspective, asphalt lines drawn along a gigantic ruler. Celia looked out her car window to where she had hoped to retrace Djuna's path through the woods. She gaped at the office plaza where the forest once had been.

CHAPTER 13

The Jensenville Library inhabited the former home of the late William Jensen in what had once been the posh part of town, a street of three-story brick mansions limping into the twenty-first century in various states of subdivision and decay. Verandas and multiple chimneys, cupolas and Palladian windows adorned crumbling brick facades like heirloom jewelry on the exhausted skins of dowager aunts. Former ballrooms, dining rooms, and conservatories had been divvied up between doctors' offices and real estate brokers, hairdressers and insurance agents. Among the subdivided was the orthodontist Celia had visited to have her braces tightened. Once every three weeks for two and a half years, Celia had walked the ten blocks from middle school to his office, and from there to the library where Noreen would pick her up. With the abrupt intensity of an acid flashback Celia recalled the sphincter-tightening revulsion of being made to bite into the soft, thick wax for the dental mold. Preserved was the view of poorly shaved Adam's apple from the reclining dental chair, the orthodontist leaning over to apply dull force to her molar, the sound of his ministrations conducted through the bones of her skull. Dr. Krantz. His name was Dr. Krantz. As Celia now passed through the library's front door, her upper jaw ached like a phantom limb.

Though the town founder's good intentions were abundantly indicated by the plaque neighboring his life-sized statue in the library vestibule—"I give this, my house, as a repository of knowledge for the city of Jensenville, so that it might become as a second home to hungry minds"—the reality was that the place felt less like a second home than an overstuffed closet. Aside from the front entry's mullioned windows, every other aperture had come to be blocked by additional bookshelves. Post-Jensen-era fluorescent light fixtures hummed along the length and breadth of plaster ceilings. Celia made for the side room, but the reference librarian's desk had been replaced by a row of computer stations. The face of the late William Jensen bounced sedately within the glowing rectangle of each monitor's blue screen.

At this time on a weekday morning, the library was refuge to the retired, the unemployed, and the unemployable. At a far table, a middle-aged man in a polyester sports coat and a tie the length and width of a cow's tongue examined a book with malign suspicion; through a doorway, a woman held an *Us* magazine in one hand while using the other to suspend a bottle over a stroller at the level of her sleeping infant's mouth.

"Excuse me," called a voice behind her. "Would you like to sign up for computer time?"

Celia turned. The librarian of her childhood had been a cardiganed creature of onionskin, a pair of glasses secured to its neck by the same-caliber chain that tethered a pen to a bank service counter. This one had elaborate enamel earrings, no glasses, and a silk blouse slightly unbuttoned.

"I was looking for the reference desk," Celia said.

The librarian laughed louder than seemed professionally appropriate. "Then I guess you haven't been here in a while," she said. "It's over there now." She gestured Celia to a different corner. Where Celia remembered racks of newspapers was the familiar thick-legged fundament of solid, dark wood—a desk fierce enough to hush raucous children.

"It took two burly guys and a heavy-duty furniture dolly to move it," the librarian explained. "Where it used to be, there are leg impressions all the way through the carpet and into the floor. I could have gotten a new desk, but this one always seemed so ideally referential. Plus, it let me blow my furniture budget on a really cool chair." She walked behind the desk and settled into something self-consciously ergonomic. "Now, how can I help you?"

"I was hoping to find information on a local street."

"If it's technical, you might need Public Works over at City

Hall," the librarian advised, "but we've got maps here, plus I'm a native Jensenvillian."

Her smile, both eager and apologetic, was what passed for civic pride.

"When I was a kid," Celia began, "my bus drove along a small wooded road to get to school. I'm pretty sure it was called Ripley."

"I thought so!" The librarian beamed. "I can always tell the ones who come back."

Celia flinched.

"You're probably just home to see your folks," she added. "Where do you live now?"

"Chicago," Celia said, tempted to produce her driver's license as proof.

The librarian nodded. "Such a shame about that road." She sighed. "No more forest primeval. Ripley got expanded back when CompuDisc came to town, and they couldn't exactly put it back the way it was after the Internet bubble burst." She studied Celia's face. "When were you at Jensenville Elementary?"

"Until '86."

The face before her brightened. "Did you know a girl named Betsy Jorgenson? She would have been a grade or two above you. She's my little sister, though she's Betsy Harris now. She did like I'm assuming you did and went away for college. That's the only way to guarantee your escape."

"A girl named Betsy?" Celia echoed.

"Long blond braids? Queen of the recess four-square set?"

"I don't think so," Celia said.

"I suppose it was a long time ago."

The fluorescents buzzed softly above.

"Um, about Ripley Road," Celia tried. "When they took down all the trees?"

"Wouldn't it have been great if they'd found the wizard's house? Or was it supposed to have been a witch?" Speech caused the librarian's earrings to collide with the side of her neck. "I tell you, I don't know what little kids do now when they want to scare the pants off of each other. I suppose there's still the abandoned inebriate asylum off Route 17, but that's a bit out of their league, don't you think?"

Celia stared.

"I'm not always this gabby," the librarian said. "It's just so nice to talk to someone who isn't constructing a conspiracy theory or watching videos of home accidents on YouTube. Was there something specific you were wondering about?"

"I just happened to be driving down Ripley, and I started thinking about that girl who disappeared back when we were kids—"

"Oh my god!" The librarian's earrings spasmed. "I absolutely remember that! Wait a minute, it'll come to me . . . Her name was J-something: Jessie, Julie, Jenna—"

"Djuna," Celia said.

"That's right! Djuna! Djuna P—" The librarian paused, then snapped her fingers. "Djuna Parson!"

"Pearson."

"She was abducted from there, wasn't she? Now that's something I haven't thought of in eons. I think my father helped with one of the search parties. For a while, I actually kept a milk carton with her face on it, until my mother found it and threw it away." She paused. "You know, I bet we knew each other. I bet if we traded photos from back then, we would recognize who we used to be."

Beside the librarian's desk was a small reference shelf holding a dictionary, a thesaurus, a world atlas, and the local white and yellow pages. "Excuse me," Celia said, and made for the door leading to the basement.

"You'll need the key if you want to use the ladies," the librarian called.

The sight of the phone directories had spurred a memory in Celia that was confirmed by the reverberation of the stairwell door closing behind her. She and Djuna had made a contest of seeing who could jump from the higher stair to the basement landing, their shoes exploding against the floor with a sound that shamed the thud of the door. The librarian—the childhood model—had never tried to investigate the noise. Whether she hadn't heard or simply considered the bookless territory of the stairwell to be beyond her jurisdiction was unclear. Her negligence, deliberate or not, had created an inside version of the untended grass beside the electrical box on Djuna's block. The railing felt low to Celia now, and the stairs were more worn, but when Celia jumped to the landing, the sound was the same. The forgotten pleasure of making noise in a quiet place was followed by the same, unadulterated feeling of triumph when no librarian came.

The steps had been prologue to their assault on the pay phone, which Djuna fed with change repurposed from a pewter mug Mr. Pearson kept on his desk. Library bathroom traffic was sparse, and the slam of the stairwell door gave ample warning of someone's approach. Because Celia refused to talk, she was in charge of choosing phone numbers, her fingers walking the slopes of the library's white pages in search of promising last names.

"Hello?" Djuna would begin. "My name is Nadine," or Scarlet, or Francesca, "and I'm in ninth grade." Ninth was the oldest Djuna thought she could manage; she pitched her voice low and overenunciated everything. "I was wondering if I could ask you some questions for a report I'm doing on trends in our community?"

Strangers seemed to enjoy helping a student with a school assignment. Djuna would angle the top part of the handset away from her ear, so that Celia could listen in. Sometimes a child would answer. Sometimes they could tell by the voice that it was someone very old. Most of the time, Djuna would ask a few questions—*How many children do you have? How many pets? How many televisions? What breakfast cereal do you eat?*—before hanging up, but sometimes she would squeeze Celia's arm. "What color is your underwear?" she would ask, her nails digging into Celia's skin. Djuna would laugh as a dial tone replaced the person at the end of the line, but once a voice had answered back.

"Blue," it had said. "I've got blue boxers on, and you have the sweetest, sexiest little voice that I have ever heard." Djuna had hung up, grinning, and Celia had told her never to do that again. In lieu of an answer, Djuna had fished out her house key from inside her shirt and scratched her initial into the side of the phone; and that was the last time Celia had gone to the library with Djuna.

Celia couldn't remember when she'd last seen a pay phone, an era having lapsed beneath her notice. Despite having entered the stairwell for no other purpose, she was still surprised to find the library's model still clinging to the same wall between restroom doors. It too was lower than Celia remembered. She had to bend sideways to see it, but the "D" was still there.

CHAPTER 14

The police were headquartered where downtown became the east side, an area shunned by Jensenville's occasional fleeting attempts at renewal, due to the lack of anything there worth renewing. Celia drove past a Laundromat and a pawnshop, a fried chicken franchise and a bowling alley. The train tracks lay to the north, now used only for freight. Talk of Amtrak resuming passenger service came in cycles usually linked to local elections or increases in property taxes, a one-sided conversation that never mentioned the steady decline of Jensenville's population in the thirty years since the train line's demise.

The police station squatted at one end of a pocked parking lot, a brick bunker stacked regular as Legos. No one passed in or out in the five minutes Celia sat staring through her wind-shield. She tried to persuade herself that the station might be closed for lunch, which gave her the fortitude to exit her car. What had seemed like a natural next step at the library had degenerated, on the drive over, into something more ques-tionable. She and Huck had discussed when to talk to the police, and this was not it: she was to first consult a lawyer. But all Celia wanted was information. She wouldn't even have to tell them her name.

The front door opened with an ease that ridiculed the notion a police station ever closed. Celia wondered at the sta-tistical probability that someone, at that very moment, was slip-ping a drugstore lipstick into her purse or running a red light. She wondered how many Jensenville crimes, large and small, went undetected, how many people passed through this door with something to hide.

Stepping inside, Celia was ambushed by homesickness. The station resembled the city agencies that filled the Bilandic, their interiors having dispensed with the need to impress, their cus-tomers guaranteed. For the first time since flying east she was reminded of her empty desk at the Auditor General's office, the one to which she would be returning in a matter of days. It was a pleasant shock to realize that her life in Chicago had not been redacted by her mother's smiley-faced good morning notes or her father's trisyllabic *hel-loo-oo*, that by having partaken of Noreen's Chicken à la Queen she was not condemned to remain. By day's end, Huck's disembodied voice would be embodied again. On Sunday evening, the two of them would trade Jensenville for a Chicago-bound plane. Celia's relief at this briefly eclipsed the fact that she'd be taking Djuna with her, that this process she'd begun had an indeterminate end.

When the police officer manning the front desk saw her, his face flashed surprise.

"Can I help you?" he said.

"Good morning," she began. The universe of her Chicago life contracted to a pinprick of distant light. "I was wondering if I could ask you a question about a local road." She felt wobbly. She was certain her face looked funny, that her voice sounded off. When she lowered herself into a metal folding chair against a nearby wall, its front legs hesitated before accepting her weight.

"Be careful on that thing," the policeman said. "You're skinny, so it'll probably be all right, but it's been known to give out on people." He gestured toward his desk, his navy blue uniform the only office fixture that wasn't gray or brown. "There's a better one over here. You want some water?" Small eyes beneath a low hairline created the impression of an overfriendly badger.

"I'm okay," Celia said and moved closer. Her new chair was identical to the first. "I'm sorry to bother you, but I'm just back visiting my parents and I was driving on Ripley Road—"

The officer shook his head. "If you want to protest a speeding ticket, you've got to wait for your day in court. If it was me, I'd just pay. I know that road, there's signs all over the place."

"It's nothing like that," Celia said. "I was hoping someone could tell me about when they made the road wider."

The policeman's brow furrowed. "Oh man, you mean

back when CompuDisc came in?" He eyed Celia as if he were running her license plate. "That's kind of a while back, don't you think?"

"Were you here then?" she asked. "When they cut down all those trees?"

Taped to a nearby wall, a green-and-purple girl rendered in Magic Marker hovered above the words *Proud to Be Drug Free*, penned in uneven rainbow letters.

The officer smiled. "You're Celia Durst, aren't you?"

All the saliva in Celia's mouth instantly vanished.

The policeman slapped his desk. "You *are* Celia! I was pretty sure it was you when you walked in, but I didn't want to say anything until I was a hundred percent positive."

"I'm sorry," she said, her voice a whisper, "but how do you—"

The officer linked his thumbs and flapped his fingers. "Fly high and away with the Jensenville Jays!" he crowed, his hands rising into the air. "Junior year, we both had third-period history with Mrs. Babbitt, the Great Unshaven. I sat in the back row and never said anything. Unlike you. You were always saying such smart things." He shook his head. "Celia Durst. You know, my brother had the biggest crush on you."

"Really?" She tried to smile.

He nodded. "He totally wanted to ask you out. Spent a week working on a note to put in your locker and at the last minute chickened out. I think he still regrets it." He offered his hand. "Mitchell Gryzbowski, at your service."

"Officer Gryzbowski—"

"Call me Mitch."

"Um, okay." Celia opened her mouth and closed it before trying again. "Um, I was wondering if there was anything on record about Ripley Road from the time it got widened." She no longer had any clue why she had thought this was a good idea.

Gryzbowski was twirling a pencil between the fingers of his right hand—pointer to middle to ring to pinkie and back again—a seamless interlocking series of figure eights. "You're thinking of the Pearson case, aren't you? Hey, don't look so shocked. That's major history around here. That was in what, '85? '86? I remember the signs posted all over town when I was a kid. Later, when I joined the force, I heard the inside dope from Frank. It was funny, joining up and then hearing your name. You remember him? Frank DiNado? He was the one who interviewed you and the other three. My guess is that he would have had you calling him Officer Frank. He was captain around here when I was a rookie."

Celia shook her head.

"Face like a hound dog? Big ears? Brown, droopy eyes?"

Celia shrugged. "I was pretty young."

Gryzbowski nodded. "I guess you blocked it out, huh? Well, he sure didn't. His biggest professional regret was never finding the son of a bitch who took her. There was no NCMEC back then, no AMBER Alert system. Just Frank putting out the word about a guy in a brown sedan. Hey, it doesn't bother you, me talking about this, does it?"

Celia closed her eyes.

"Because you're looking pale again. You want a piece of gum?"

He retrieved a pack of something sugarless and berry-flavored. Celia smiled but didn't move.

Gryzbowski shrugged. "I gave up smoking when I got divorced. Figured as long as I was miserable I might as well break up with cigarettes too. I used to chew four packs a day, but now I'm down to one." He laughed. "That's progress, right? Here, let me at least get you some water." He walked to a dispenser and returned with a paper cup.

"Thank you," she said. She thought she might be ready to try again. "When they tore down the trees . . ."

"Right, right," Gryzbowski said. "Ripley Road. Now that *was* my time. '98, '97, something like that. A few nature freaks had a petition going around, but I was glad to see that road widened. There were always teenagers speeding on that thing, too many of them wrapping their cars around trees. You wanted to know if they found anything when they tore it up, but there wouldn't have been anything to find. Those woods got searched like crazy back when it happened. After the Pearson girl got snatched, they had the K-9 unit out there; they had state troopers; they had volunteer search parties. Frank had real mixed feelings about them putting in the throughway. Ripley was his last link to the case, and I'm not sure he was ready to give that up. He retired from the force a few years back, moved out to Arizona. Not a bad plan, if you ask me. I've been thinking that I might be just about done with Jensenville, you know? It might be time for me to turn over a bunch of new leaves."

Gryzbowski leaned back and stretched his arms behind his

head, revealing darker ovals at the underarms of his shirt. He peered at Celia over the length of his elongated body. "So tell me, Celia Durst, where did you go to leave all this behind?"

"Chicago," she said. Two other desks were empty. Through a door, she could hear a voice talking into a phone. She turned toward the entry, as if looking might conjure someone else.

"Chicago, huh? That's on a lake, right? I think I might be able to live in a city if it was next to a lake." He retracted himself and leaned across the ravaged surface of his desk. "Look, you wouldn't happen to be free for dinner, would you? I could take you to a real nice Italian place in Maynard. You could tell me what Chicago's all about."

Her short, sharp laugh was like a wayward belch. "I don't think so," she said, her voice an octave higher. "My boyfriend—"

Gryzbowski's blunt fingers waved the question away. "Hey, I didn't see a ring so I figured it couldn't hurt to ask. I've got to level with you, Celia. The guy with the crush back in high school was me."

"Oh," she said. "Well, that's very flattering—"

"But totally inappropriate. One of my professional weaknesses. Forget I said anything. And sorry I couldn't give you better news about Ripley Road. Though if you ask me, the creep who took the Pearson girl would never have put her back where he found her."

"What about a hole?" she asked, the words rushing out of her.

"A what?"

"A hole." She considered turning around and walking out. "Like an old, abandoned well?" She tried to think of a way to put it that wouldn't give herself away. "What if—what if he dumped her there and then left her," she said. "What if he did it after the search parties were done, after there was no one looking for her anymore?"

Gryzbowski shook his head. "Now you're beginning to sound like Frank," he said with something like admiration. "Years later, he was still going over all the angles. I bet it was hard, huh? A nice girl like you, losing a friend like that at such a tender age?"

He leaned closer.

"Let me tell you something about this sort of crime," he said. "It's a crime of opportunity. A guy like that sees a girl, and maybe he's been looking for a girl for a while, or maybe he sees her and something just snaps inside him, but he takes her, okay? After that, one of three things happens: he either kills her— usually after doing completely fucked up, animal things to her—or he keeps her tucked away somewhere—a basement, or even a tent in his backyard—or he sells her. I tell my daughter: someone sketchy tries to talk to you, scream 'No!' and run away. Don't wait to hear what they're going to say." He shook his head. "That Pearson girl didn't stand a chance. If he killed her, I suppose she could have turned up in the woods, but then we would have found her. Maybe not right away, maybe not for years, even, but let me tell you, if there had ever been anything to find, Frank would have found it."

"But when they widened the road," Celia persisted, "what if Frank didn't think to—"

She was stopped by the look on Mitch Gryzbowski's face.

"Captain DiNado was the finest police officer I ever had the privilege to know. And if anyone ever tries to tell you otherwise . . ." Gryzbowski shook his head. "He sacrificed himself for the force," he said. "And I mean *sacrificed*, okay? To this day it haunts him that little girl was never found. Frank DiNado is a haunted man."

Something fierce in him flared and then died.

Celia stood, bracing herself against the chair for support. "Well," she said softly, "thank you for your time."

Gryzbowski smiled. "Celia Durst," he said. "The pleasure was all mine. I'm going to tell Frank that I saw you. He'll be happy to know that you turned out all right." She thought at first he was waving but it was just his pencil, slicing empty circles into the air.

CHAPTER 15

She drove along the commercial drag of Jensenville's east side, calmed by four lanes of sparse traffic brought to its knees by untimed stoplights. No ghosts of Djuna haunted the carpet emporium or the trailer home dealership, the Salvation Army thrift store or the fabric outlet. Each was heralded by an out-sized parking lot whose dimensions were magnified by a dearth of parked cars. Sidewalks were sandwiched by skimpy lines of ailing grass, interrupted at cruelly irregular intervals by bus stops whose patrons wore long-distance stares, their stillness not a show of patience but of abject dependence on a bus that had not come. Until Celia saw the sign, the anonymity of this landscape was a tonic, a space to clear her brain.

The paint job had faded but was otherwise unchanged, PAULI'S SPIEDIES stacking itself vertically beside a painted meat skewer of massive proportion. Each individual pork cube was the size of a mastiff, the area's sole native delicacy puncturing the horizon like an admonishing finger. Celia had been here before. This had been Leanne's part of town, Pauli's passed on the way to a birthday party reconstituted from memory's slurry of hats, paper tablecloths, and balloons. Leanne's had been a throwback to the old model. By fifth grade it was nearly all sleepovers, girls in nightgowns circling one another chanting, "Light as a feather, stiff as a board." The only partygoer aside from the four of them had been a neighbor in a Boy Scout uniform who did little more than silently glare at them from across the room. Leanne's mother had spent the party patting their shoulders, repeating how happy she was to meet her daughter's girlfriends. Celia remembered the chemical smell of the plastic furniture covers; a kitchen nook from which Mrs. Forrest had produced a homemade cake; an aging photo of a sallow-skinned, pink-swaddled baby beside Leanne's school portrait in the living room, *Heaven's Littlest Angel* engraved on its tarnished frame. Leanne's house was a revelation, the first kitchen/family room combo Celia had ever seen, and no dining room at all. Had the baby sister lived, she would have had to bunk with Leanne in the bedroom Celia glimpsed in a reconnaissance mission disguised as a bathroom foray, a bedroom not much bigger than the single child's bed it contained. Celia had only ever passed houses like Leanne's on her way somewhere else. She'd never thought of them as inhabited, certainly not by anyone she knew. Leanne's birthday party represented the first time Celia's own good fortune slapped her across the face.

Huck was arriving that afternoon. Their plan called for him to rent a car at the terminal to spare Celia's parents the need to chauffeur them back to the airport on Sunday. This had made sense when they'd had no particular need to be alone. Celia stayed on Commerce Road just long enough to reach the turn-off for the Syracuse-bound lanes of Route 81.

Huck's time in Baltimore, during their relationship's precocious infancy, had been one of the last summers in the history of young love to rely on the postal service. Huck's envelopes had been covered with doodles, Celia's with carefully selected stamps. Huck wrote on a napkin from Bertha's Mussels; Celia enclosed sand from North Beach. She'd scouted the mailbox with the earliest pickup time, walking five extra blocks in case that might shave three hours off her letter's East Coast arrival. By surprising Huck now, the two of them would be gaining ninety minutes, more if Celia told her parents they had hit highway traffic. After seventy-five miles, the silhouette of the airport's control tower appeared in Celia's windshield like a lighthouse calling her stray ship home.

He was not expecting her and so was not looking, having resigned himself to the loneliness of airports. Before Celia could discern features, she gleaned his lean shoulders and lanky arms from Terminal A's stream of arrivals. The escalator's descent brought the square jaw into view, the indefatigable cowlick, Huck's hand resting on the moving rail as if he had been born at a 30-degree angle. Even the stillness imposed by a crowded escalator looked good on him, the only passenger who did not glance down to finesse his first, resumptive step. Celia could no sooner unlearn how to read than lose her ability to spot Huck at a distance, even were she to stop being the one he returned to. She had come, in part, to see what would happen when she stepped into his line of sight, if his face would still trade its public expression for one she thought of as hers alone: the eyes widening, the pupils dilating, the nostrils flaring as if picking up a familiar scent. When Huck spotted her, his eyebrows arched in concert with the corners of his mouth, prelude to the wide, goofy grin that was the purest, most timeless expression of his delight, a circus and ice-cream-cone holdover minted in boyhood and kept in circulation ever since. Huck's face flushed from the uptick in his pulse. His gaze claimed Celia as the person he knew best. Their eyes acknowledged their mutual expertise, no society more elite, a club capped at two. Celia called Huck's name. She grasped his shoulders and pulled herself in. They were the same height, their lips the most natural conjunction. A kiss in an airport is like an orange in the desert.

"You surprised me."

"This buys us some time," she said. "I couldn't imagine marching straight into the den with my folks and acting as if—"

"Kiss me again," he said.

Celia was uncomfortable with public displays, even in the sanctioned zone of Arrivals. Huck liked romantic tableaus. Their compromise was a second kiss slightly shorter than the first, followed by the clasping of hands.

"I'm glad you came," he said.

She knew his clothes would be fresh for the flight in order to be worn again tomorrow, that his blue carry-on contained everything he deemed necessary: one additional outfit, a small bag of toiletries, a book, CDs for the road. She sought refuge in these small certainties.

"How were the girls when you left?" she asked.

"Impossible," he said. "You know how they were all week, so you can imagine what it was like trying to take them to the kennel."

"Weren't you going to pay Jenna extra to do weekend walks?" she asked.

"I was," he said, "only she wasn't sure she'd be able to do two on Sunday and the girls were already so mopey from you not being around that I decided I didn't want to freak them out any more by leaving them alone in the apartment. I took them to that fancy place with the indoor and outdoor play areas. Bella perked up as soon as she saw the other dogs, but Sylvie gave me the dirtiest look."

"Poor Sylvie." Celia sighed. "She probably hates me by now."

"Nah," Huck said. "She's still crazy about you."

A sliding glass door released them from the terminal's canned air into an environment that transmitted actual weather. They crossed to the parking garage, a breeze tugging at them like an exuberant child. Reunion and sex offered similar comforts. Time-honored habits created a temporary sanctuary from what was new or in doubt, a place where everything was as it had always been.

"You've got your mom's car?" Huck asked. "Right, stupid question. He just got a new one, didn't he?"

"Didn't I tell you? This one's silver."

"Oh right, with the moonroof! Well, would you mind driving then? I don't trust that weird lumbar thing your mom swears by."

Celia nodded as if this were a spontaneous decision, as if they had not both already known she'd be behind the wheel. Huck's innate grace was a localized phenomenon, a physical currency that turned to buttons outside his body's domain. Objects held or worn—a guitar, skates, a carving knife—were subject to his mastery, but anything larger—a bicycle, a car— left him artless. Huck's late entry into automotive life kept him to the far right-hand lanes, rigidly observing the speed limit as every other car passed him by. For Celia, who had been driving since she was sixteen, being Huck's passenger was an exercise in managed frustration. They maintained the illusion of shared driving less for Huck's ego than for the sake of their relationship's equitability. The housework was split between them, the mortgage jointly held. During their first months of cohabitation they had regularly switched places in bed, but the practicality of His and Hers—bastion of personal reading preferences, nocturnal hygiene regimens, and sleep aids— finally overrode Huck's fear of becoming his parents. Equity, they came to realize, was not the same thing as equivalence, as evidenced by bedside tables and snowflakes the world over.

Route 81 offered vistas of forest and hill, the water views south of Syracuse giving way to barn silos and plowed fields.

Huck slid back the front passenger seat to prop his heels on his end of the dashboard, the soles of his sneakers pressed against the windshield's interior glass. It was his preferred road trip position, which he made look so natural that Celia had once tried it for five seconds before discovering how ridiculously uncomfortable it was for anyone else. Across the front seat, the two of them traded five days of half-remembered dreams and short-lived discomforts, small felicities and minor setbacks, minutiae that proximity made pertinent again. Huck's intensity as he spoke was something Celia had first known in her father, but which maturity had allowed her to find sexy when transposed. Huck teased that they could have been spared years of heartache had they met earlier, but Celia disagreed. Her prior love life had been too binary, the replication or repudiation of her parents consuming its earliest daisy petals. Had they met any sooner, Celia might have tossed Huck away.

By Huck's time, Celia had come to accept that passion was an inborn trait like perfect pitch or a photographic memory, easy to admire and impossible to cultivate. Physical passion wasn't enough. She envied her father's ardor for bebop, Huck's zeal as he described the satirical writings of Benjamin Franklin. Growing up, she had mocked Jeremy's serial obsessions—dinosaurs, Greek mythology, and Middle-Earth giving way to Gene Simmons and Trent Reznor—while secretly coveting an avocation of her own. The unpredictability of Djuna's passions had been part of her appeal: anything that happened to catch her eye was fair game. In retrospect Celia realized their friendship had been the first in a long series of misguided chicken-pox parties in which she had attempted through close and repeated contact to catch something wholly incommunicable. Not until the trouble with Jeremy had Celia finally understood the value of a stolid temperament like her own that sought, instead, to bask in reflected light.

Celia had been watching the odometer since gaining the highway. It suddenly seemed that seventy-five miles—now sixty-eight—was a distance she would much rather savor as she had their airport reunion, seeking refuge in vacation scenery and the familiar rhythms of the road.

"So let's talk," Huck said, and Celia's stomach clenched. Huck slid forward to align his body with hers and removed his feet from the windshield, leaving two sunlit tread marks behind.

The odometer marked the demise of one more mile.

"What's wrong?" he asked. "All the blood just drained from your face."

"I guess I'm a little nervous."

"Why?"

"When I was waiting for you at the airport . . ." She shook her head. "I wasn't sure whether seeing you would be the same, but then it was. It was just like it had always been. And I know that should have felt good, but when we were walk-ing to the car, I started thinking, what if this is the last time?" She pulled to the side of the road.

"Ceel," he said.

She squeezed the wheel to steady herself, stared ahead to where the highway met the sky.

"Look at me, Ceel. After last night, do you really think—"

"But the thing is, I can't remember when we last did that! I don't mean on the phone. It's been . . ." She shook her head.

"It's been a long time," he said.

"And so when we hung up, I started thinking. I didn't want to, but I couldn't help it, about the ways that people say good-bye."

Huck stared. "Is that what you want?"

When she touched his cheek, she realized that he had shaved for her at some point before boarding the plane. "No," she said. "But you've been unhappy, and we've been so . . . I don't even mean this week. I mean before."

Huck leaned across the seat and kissed her. The warmth of his face graced her cheeks, her chin, the skin of her closed eyes. "That was not a good-bye kiss," he said.

Cars passed them in bursts of sound.

"Tell me what's been going on," he said.

"There's just so much." Celia closed her eyes. "There's us, and then there's Djuna, and there's being at home, and each one feels like it's hovering . . ."

Huck reached for her shoulder. "Start with today. There's at least twelve hours I need to get caught up on. The rest . . ." He shrugged. "We'll take the rest as it comes."

"This morning," Celia said, "I went back to Ripley Road. I hadn't gone there since elementary school, but it's stayed in my head ever since."

Hearing the timbre of her voice, Celia recognized the ridiculous weight of that morning's disappointment. The vanishment of the woods and all it had contained was a page torn from childhood's portfolio of impotence, that stunning array of rained-out field trips, poorly timed illnesses, and adult interventions that provided constant proof of one's inconsequence to the larger world.

"To get there, I drove the route the school bus used to take," she explained. "Everything matched my memory until I got to the last turn. Ripley used to be this twisty, wooded road barely two lanes wide, no lane markings, no side rails. Now it's four straight lanes of traffic with an office building where the forest used to be."

The scene outside Huck's passenger-side window embodied what Celia had been hoping to find—trees stretching miles into the distance, a panoply of green. In her child's memory, the unsullied forest bordering Ripley Road had marked the edge of the known world.

"Everything was gone?" Huck asked.

"Everything," she echoed. "It might sound silly, but I was positive I'd be able to retrace Djuna's path. I was sure I remembered which curve it had been, what road signs it was near. I'd been counting on those woods still being there."

Huck nodded. "You wanted closure."

"No." The word ricocheted off the windshield, amplifying the sound of Celia's exasperation. The day's dashed hopes had temporarily reduced her to the childish presumption that someone she loved should, in return for that love, be able to read her mind. "I wanted proof," she said. "A girl disappearing after a fall doesn't sound nearly as convincing as a girl disappearing after getting into a stranger's car—which is why I knew I had to find the well."

Voicing the words felt like loosing a small, frail-limbed child into the world.

"I remember you mentioning a well on the phone," Huck said.

"An abandoned well," she corrected. "And stop looking at me like that."

"Like what?"

"I don't know. Like I'm made of some kind of fragile material you're checking for cracks."

Huck sighed. "You're talking to me, Celia. When you talk to me, I look at you."

"I know. I just really want for you to believe me."

"Tell me about the well," he coaxed. "The abandoned well, I mean."

"I keep going over it in my mind and it's the only thing that makes sense. There's no reason there couldn't have been a well left over from when someone had lived in those woods, or from when the land had been part of a larger estate. That would account for the suddenness of it, why Djuna wouldn't have been able to make a sound or get back up after she fell."

"And that's what you were hoping to find."

She didn't like how soft his voice had become. "That's not crazy, is it? I mean, if the woods hadn't been cut down, the well might have still been there. I could have brought Becky, or Leanne, or Josie, or even my parents. Anyone who needed to be shown."

"And you don't think," he said slowly, "that the police

would have found something like that before? Back when Djuna first disappeared and there were all those searches?"

Celia tightened her grip on the wheel. "It's not like I haven't considered that," she said. "And no, Huck, I don't."

They returned to the road, Celia's jaw clenching and unclenching, Huck gently chewing his lower lip.

"So then, what do you think happened?" he finally asked. "To the well, I mean."

"I think it got filled in," she said. "Either when they were widening the road or sometime before. If it happened before, it might have been a rushed job and they might not have even looked inside. And even if it was done right, and they cleared it out before filling it in, there'd be no reason to think anything would have been left for them to find. Not if they weren't looking. Not if the hole had been open to the elements all that time, if there'd been standing water."

From the corner of her eye, she thought she saw him nod.

"Have you shared this theory with your parents?" he asked.

"I just drove out there this morning," she said. "Plus, I don't want to tell them anything until I know I can convince them. With the woods gone, that means I'll need to wait until after I've talked to Josie or Leanne."

Her jaw ached as if she'd spent hours chewing gum. She couldn't tell if she sounded reasonable or desperate.

"What about tomorrow," Huck asked, "when your brother is here?"

"I'm still waiting to hear back from Mrs. Linke," she said.

"I'm hoping to talk to both Josie and Leanne before I visit Djuna's mother. So, I'm thinking I'll visit Leanne before brunch tomorrow, and save Mrs. Pearson for the end of the day."

"You mean your e-mail campaign with Leanne actually worked?"

"No," Celia said. "But I know where she lives."

"Wait." Huck shook his head. "You can't just show up. I mean, it took you twenty-one years to deal with this. Don't you think Leanne deserves more than a couple days?"

"I can't stand the idea of her being so close," Celia said. "If I went back to Chicago without trying to see her, it would torture me. She might move or we might fall out of touch, and then I'd spend the rest of my life regretting that I hadn't tried when I had the chance."

Celia could feel Huck looking at her again. She feigned absorption in the road until he looked away.

"What do we do in the meantime?" he said. "This evening with your folks, for instance?"

"The same as always. We'll eat and then watch cable until Mommy and Daddy go to bed."

"But won't it be unbearable?" he persisted. "All that sitting around together, not saying anything?"

She shrugged. "It's what we do."

The passing towns—Onondaga, Skaneateles, Assembly Park, Slab City—were testaments to what had been or had come to be. It occurred to Celia that Syracuse was roughly as far north along I-81 as Scranton was south. A comprehensive driving map of the past few days would resemble six o'clock on a slightly eccentric watch face, with Jensenville at its center.

"Here comes Killawog," Huck said. The names formed a familiar litany, a string of towns that only ever led to one destination.

CHAPTER 16

The sight of Jensenville's stone arch through the passenger-side window comforted Huck like the opening credits of a movie made familiar from frequent television airings. He wasn't so intimate with Main Street as to know the exact arc of its commercial decline, but he had memorized the static contour of its skyline. Huck found it hard not to love the way Jensenville had aged. It was one of those time-capsule towns whose prosperity had been bestowed in a single lightning strike of good fortune and had dissipated just as quickly, leaving red-brick mansions with mansard roofs; the cupola atop City Hall; the wide, curved windows of the downtown storefronts; and the opera house with its stone tower. Writ larger, Jensenville could have been a Pittsburgh, PA; smaller, and it could have been a Portsmouth, NH—all civic versions of the uncannily preserved corpse disinterred from the muck of a peat bog. Jensenville was an American fossil, a triumph of early twentieth-century industrialism set adrift in the twenty-first, emblem of an extinct age when factories begot cities.

Since falling silent at the 81 turnoff, Huck had been staring at the passing scenery, Celia drumming her fingers on the wheel. "What are you thinking about?" he asked.

"My parents should be home by now," she said. "It's been weird, me being here without you. They're not used to it."

"They miss me." Huck sighed.

"They do," she agreed. "Plus, I think they want to pump you for information."

"What should I tell them?"

She shrugged. "Tell them whatever you want."

As they passed the corner of Brahms and Hoffman, Huck was hazy on his exact relation to Schubert, but could have steered them in the right general direction. After years of walking tours, Huck knew the major landmarks: the former home of Celia's bulimic babysitter; the corner where the kid with Down syndrome had stood for hours at a time, waving at passing cars. On a bench in Jensen Park, Celia had launched their only-ever public make-out session, explaining afterward that they had exorcised her memory of Harlan Posner, whose slobber had choked her on that very spot in eighth grade. With that, Huck had thought he'd been told everything there was to know.

Yesterday evening, he realized that he'd been treating his

solitude as a trial run. Mornings were a rush, then there was
school, and even coming home at the end of the day to Bella
and Sylvie had felt no different than before. Only in the hour
following the dogs' walk did loneliness assume Celia's name,
but Huck's trouble distinguishing habit from need was an old,
old problem, and one not limited to people. Though he would
have never admitted it to Celia—he could barely admit it
to himself—part of the thrill of their phone call later that night
had been that once they got started, it could have been anyone
on the other end of the line.

He would not go so far as to say that Celia's surprise
appearance at the airport had saved something, but Huck
wasn't sure how else he might have achieved the clarity of that
moment. He had spotted her at the base of the escalator and
recognition had spiked him to his marrow, an electric jolt pro-
claiming to his every cell and particle that he was hers alone.
She'd been watching him the whole time, waiting until he saw
her before calling his name, to let him see the shape of it in her
mouth.

"I bet they were posting lookout from the living room,"
she said as she pulled the car into the driveway. "Prepare yourself. Mommy came back from the store with, like, six bags of
groceries."

Warren and Noreen were hovering at the edge of the
walk. Huck could not look at them without seeing a complex
series of addends: Noreen's hair + Noreen's lips + Warren's
stature + Warren's chin = Celia. Huck appreciated such genetic
transparency for the glimpse it gave him of his future. Noreen's
hair was becoming wispier, the skin of Warren's chin had loos-

ened, and they were both thicker in the waist, details that had helped Huck to picture himself at Celia's side in the decades to come.

"Huck, it's so nice to see you," Noreen said. Her hug, which took in his shoulders but left space between their torsos, was followed by a kiss to the cheek and three pats to the back.

"Hello there, Huck." Warren leaned in with a simultaneous back clasp and handshake. "I was telling Celia that you two should think about visiting more often when it's warm and green."

Huck nodded. "It was a beautiful drive from the airport."

Huck was a full-service greeter by nature, active disdainer of the air kiss and half hug. Filmed in black and white and set to piano, his first few visits to Jensenville could have passed for silent comedy, his physical enthusiasm capsizing the Dursts' restraint, several false starts endured in the search for a mutually comprehensible welcome. He had never seen Celia's parents touch, outside chaste kisses exchanged at Christmas. Celia once told him that she had never seen her parents' bedroom door closed; and in that brief, unwelcome moment before Huck banished Noreen and Warren's sex life from his mind, he had prayed that there were certain fates he and Celia could avoid.

They went inside. For Huck, who had grown up in a series of cramped apartments in Cleveland Heights, Celia's childhood home would never cease to feel palatial. At a party, he'd once overheard Celia joke to a friend that their apartment lacked the space for children. He thought she was hardly qualified to judge, having grown up where half a room was devoted to an uninhabitable couch. Neither could he understand why a house with space to spare would hang its family photos in the hallway. Why put pictures somewhere narrow and poorly lit, where there's no place to sit? To really look at them he had to lean against the coat closet, jamming its doorknob into the small of his back.

Stopping there now, Huck had to admit that he liked the hallway's privacy. It wasn't a place where people stuck around, which allowed him to ogle Celia's pictures without feeling self-conscious. In early studio portraits involving hobbyhorses and abstract backgrounds, her face could have foretold any number of future people, but by the time of the waterfall backdrop, the autumn trees, and the country scene, her poses bestowed protean glimpses of the woman she would become. In one, she held her head at an angle that belonged to her adult repertoire of gestures; in another, she had gained the posture that would exalt her once she became tall. Huck had no idea how the photographer had managed it, but in the fifth portrait—Celia could not have been older than ten—she showed her true smile, her frequently-sighted-but-impossible-to-capture smile, the one she could never produce on command. In it she looked so much like herself, only smaller, that Huck was seized by feelings generally considered criminal.

"Don't you ever get sick of looking at those?" Celia murmured as she passed.

"No," he replied.

He felt most comfortable in the den, which lay behind the more ceremonial living and dining rooms and off to the left, like a proper heart. Noreen had already outfitted the coffee table with the bowls of grapes and oranges, the plate of cheese and crackers, the dish of M&M's, and the half glasses of white wine—which would all conspire to make leftovers of the Japanese food they would order so painstakingly, Noreen and Warren puzzling over the dog-eared take-out menu as if it were high-order math before settling on their same old circled selections.

As he and Celia settled on the couch, Huck knew better than to reach for her hand. Early on, he had made a point of flaunting Celia's Jensenville prohibitions—stealing a kiss in the kitchen, or asking her parents direct questions about money or their health. Huck's parents didn't come with such strictures: around Alyce and Quinn, he'd always been able to do and say what he liked, an oceanic freedom that—Celia reminded him—had nearly drowned him. Her parents were different, she'd said, and if Huck truly desired their acceptance, he would respect their limitations. Rather than try to change them, he should try to understand them, advice Huck had been humbled to realize required much more effort and attention than anything he had previously attempted.

"It's funny," Warren began once dinner had been phoned in, "but we've all been so busy these past few days that we haven't really had a chance to enjoy one another." He swiveled his recliner away from the TV. "Cee Cee, if I promise to stay up until ten tonight, will you forgive your decrepit mother and me the early hours we've been keeping?"

"It's okay, Daddy," Celia said. "I'm not great company right now anyway."

He batted her words away with his hand. "You're never bad company. Is she, Huck?"

Celia flinched at being reduced to third person, which she swore her father never did with Jeremy. Only she was ever made to feel invisible.

"Sure she is, sometimes," Huck answered, then turned to Celia to break the spell. "But you have great taste in film," he told her, "and you know the rules to every card game, which in my book more than makes up for it."

Noreen appeared from the kitchen holding a bowl of cubed cantaloupe. "Melon," she announced. "You see what visiting in April gets you? I've told Celia it's a crime, depriving a Midwestern boy like yourself the beauty of a New York State spring."

"Mom." Celia sighed. "We do have melon in Chicago."

"Of course you do," Noreen agreed. She swiveled her recliner to match her husband's at a parallel angle. "A toast," she said. "To your visit."

Huck clinked. Viewed through his glass, the room closed around him in a blurred circle.

"So," Noreen began, "I suppose Celie told you the good news?"

Celia returned Huck's blank look.

"About Pam?" Noreen prompted.

"Oh," Huck said. "Yes, of course. Congratulations!" He tried nodding to lend the words more force.

"Thanks." Warren grinned. "They don't know yet if it's a girl or a boy, but I'm thinking a boy will be easier—they've already got the clothes, plus Pam grew up with brothers so she knows how to handle them."

"Oh, I don't know," Noreen demurred. "I think Pam wouldn't mind a girl. I know how much I liked having one of each."

"I'll tell you one thing." Celia's father leaned forward. "Boys and girls are different, no two ways about it. Different interests, different games—"

Noreen nodded. "It was always so easy to figure out who to invite to Jem's birthday parties, but Celie was a different story. Do you remember your slumber parties, sweetie? You used to torture yourself over who should be on or off the list."

"I sure wasn't sad to see that go," Warren said. "All that shrieking and whispering, and at some point there was always one little girl reduced to tears. Then, by middle school, it was tons of kids for pizza and a movie. They'd be sprawled over every inch of the den, eating cheese slices like they'd never been fed. Who were those kids, Cee Cee?"

Celia was silent, their talk like water around a stone. Huck tried to catch her eye but she was intent on twisting the skeletal remains of a grape cluster in her fingers, its fruit consumed, the divaricated stem in her hand like the remains of a tiny tree.

"Cee Cee?" Warren asked, and Celia looked toward her father as if startled awake. "Who were those kids who came to your pizza parties? Were they from Newspaper Club and Mock Trial, and all those other things?"

Celia shrugged. "I guess so, Daddy. I just invited anyone. Whoever came, came."

The ticking of the wall clock in the dining room combined with the muted sound of hip-hop from a neighboring yard to amplify the new silence in the den. Noreen examined her glass. Warren tapped at his armrests as if he'd adopted Morse Code.

"Well, I think it's been twenty minutes," he said. "I'd better go hunt down our sushi before it gets cold." He chuckled as he rose from his chair. "Why don't you come with me, Huck? You can see the new car in action."

In ten years of fetching their dinners, Warren had never requested Huck's company. Huck looked to Celia just as her hip pocket began to vibrate. Without a word, she rose from the couch.

Noreen asked, "Who is it?" but Celia was already in the hall.

"Ceel?" Huck called.

"It's fine, Huck," she called behind her. "Go with Daddy." She took the stairs two at a time.

CHAPTER 17

"Mrs. Linke? Thanks so much for getting back to me."

"Of course, Celia. I've got a number for you. Josie's so looking forward to catching up."

As Celia scrambled for pen and paper, she caught a glimpse of her father's departing car through the guest room window. Between thanking Mrs. Linke and hanging up, there was an awkward pause in which she sensed Josie's mother gauging whether or not to pretend at having anything more to say.

Celia looked at the ten digits she had just scrawled on a gas receipt. Josie had joined their ranks with only slightly more subtlety than Leanne, hers a dogged courtship instead of a direct appeal. Josie began wearing her hair in a ponytail, abandoning a long-term relationship with the ribbon barrette. One day she appeared in school with a jacket identical to Djuna's, asserting she'd had it forever. To woo Celia, she claimed to have always loved poetry. A notebook purportedly filled with original verse was brandished but never opened. Josie could be counted on to laugh at any joke, second any plan, or substantiate any claim. Djuna's private mockery of this made Celia thankful that Josie's bids for acceptance had upstaged her own.

After Josie's phone rang six times, Celia stopped counting. She was mentally composing a suitable voice mail when a female voice almost startled her into hanging up.

"Oh!" Celia said, standing in her excitement, a suitor hesitating at the threshold.

"Hello?" the voice repeated.

"Josie?"

Josie exclaimed Celia's name, the first syllable stretched like a piece of taffy. The sound placed Celia beside Djuna on the morning school bus, the two of them pretending to ignore Josie's arrival. Celia was struck temporarily mute. She could smell grape bubble gum and the sour reek of midweek lunch boxes.

"Is this an okay time?" she asked when she was released by that ghost of herself in shorts and matching socks, the skin of her thighs fused to a green vinyl bus seat. "Your mother said early evenings were best."

"Anytime is just fine for you!" said Josie. "Wow, Celie Durst. It's been, what, twenty years?"

"Something like that." Celia plumbed her memory for images of Josie in middle or high school but could only summon

Josie's forsaken ribbon barrettes, hair dangling from each side of her head like the ears of a cocker spaniel.

"Gosh, it doesn't seem like that long, does it?" Josie said. "Your folks are still in Jensenville, huh?"

Celia glanced at her mother's sewing table. According to the dusty stack of pattern envelopes, the last real action that corner had seen was the creation of a Han Solo costume. "Yeah. I don't think they'll ever move."

"Oh god, mine neither. We should get our parents together. They would totally hit it off." Josie sighed. "You know, I always regretted that we fell out of touch. Every few years, I would think to myself, 'I wonder what happened to Celie Durst?' but I was too scatterbrained to ever do anything about it. That's something I always admired about you, how organized you were. I bet you're a high-powered lawyer now, or some kind of corporate executive."

Celia suspected that Josie was thinking of Becky. "Nothing that fancy," she said. "I'm in Chicago. I work for the city."

"You're in Chicago?" Josie echoed. "I might be in a group show there! If it works out, I'll invite you to the opening!"

Celia's throat tightened. "I saw some of your sculptures online," she said, and waited for what would come next.

"For what it's worth," Josie said, "they always look crappy on the Internet. There's the whole problem of scale, plus the mixed-media aspects."

The figures Celia had seen had been stranded in the center of large, empty rooms or shunted into corners. "Is that stuff wax?" she asked, which felt as relevant as asking the color of someone's shirt once they had leapt off a bridge.

"Actually, it's a kind of polyester resin. I cribbed the technique from Louise Bourgeois by way of Ron Mueck. Are you familiar with those two?"

"I'm not sure." Celia visited the Art Institute for the really big shows. She tried to imagine seeing Josie's work without feeling like she had been publicly turned inside out.

"Well, there's at least one Bourgeois at the Art Institute, and Mueck was part of a group show at the MCA a few years ago . . . not that I'm keeping track." Josie laughed. "As you can see, I'm slightly competitive."

They sat at their respective ends of the line.

"Is your work always about girls?" Celia finally asked.

"Yeah, I used to feel bad about that," Josie said, "but then I read a quote by Judy Chicago about how an artist should always trust her voice. Plus, once someone called me a mixed-media, feminist Henry Darger, which totally made my day, so I decided to stop worrying."

"And is it all taken from memory?" Celia persisted. "Because the three pieces I saw—"

"The Feminettes," Josie said. "That was the first time I really let my work get personal. It felt weird, because I hate art as memoir, but for a piece to really resonate you've got to put part of yourself in there. The trick is striking the right balance. So when I decided to draw upon what happened—"

"It was all there," Celia said. "The fight Djuna and I had, the five of us on Ripley Road. But the one that really threw me was the one in the woods. I'm not sure how . . . I mean, I remember you waiting back at the road with Becky and

Leanne. I didn't see you but if you were there, if you actually *saw* what happened—"

"Uh, Celie?" Josie interrupted, and Celia realized that where her non-phone hand had been gripping the blanket, there were five fingertip-sized gaps in the weave.

"I want to apologize," Josie said. "I can only imagine what it would be like, finding that stuff out of the blue. Back when I started on those pieces, I wondered about contacting you, to ask if it was okay, but I didn't because . . . I mean, what if I asked and you said no? So in the end, I just went ahead and hoped that if you saw them, you'd see the ways in which our experience had inspired the work without telling anyone's specific story. I guess I hoped that you might feel . . . well, honored, I suppose, but the more I thought about it, the more I realized that regardless of the whole permission thing, which is complicated, I should at least have *told* you. Not to ask your blessing, but because you deserved to know. But after a while, it began to feel too late. And it's been this sort of lasting regret of mine ever since."

Celia felt her hands unclench. "Look, can I just ask you?" This was her last best chance. "How have you managed to live with what you saw? Because I'm finding it pretty hard—"

"It *was* hard," Josie said. "Which is probably why I avoided that material for so long. I wanted to think I'd put it behind me, you know? But something like that, it stays with you, it's part of the way you see the world, the way you see yourself."

Celia sprang from the bed, smiling from the relief of finally not having to explain herself. "God, it's so good to be talking like this," she said. "I mean, I thought I was the only one. But if you were there too, it means . . . well, it means that you made the same choice that I did. And . . . I can't believe I'm saying this . . . I mean, two wrongs don't make a right, but to know all these years that it hasn't just been me—"

"Oh Celie." The pity in Josie's voice stopped Celia mid-stride. "It just isn't true. I mean, I used to think that if only I had said something, maybe I could have saved her, that if only I had tried a little harder, she wouldn't have gone, but that's . . . that's magical thinking."

Celia returned to the bed.

"I can understand how you feel," Josie continued. "But the truth is that Djuna was as good as gone the second that car pulled over. Nothing we could have said or done would have stopped her."

"But there was no car," Celia said. "You know that . . . you saw for yourself, in the woods. You saw her fall, and you chose to walk away."

"In the woods?" Josie made a sound that was not quite a laugh. "I'm sorry, Celie, but I was scared just being *next* to those woods. If you went in, then you were out by the time I came around the curve. I told Becky to stay with Leanne so I could check to see what you guys had decided to do . . . Do you know that at that point, I think Leanne was actually hold-ing her own hands together and telling Becky how to retie the knots because the ones that Djuna tied had come undone?" Josie sighed. "I could never figure Leanne out. She was always so . . . willing. No matter what grade you and Djuna gave her, she always accepted it. I remember this one day: she showed up with French braids and a shirt that had puffy sleeves. And, sure, it looked a little weird on her but she had really tried, you know? I remember thinking she deserved at least a B-plus, maybe even an A-minus, but you guys gave her the same grades you always did and she just took it, the same as she took everything else. Like wearing that sign, or when you made her sit on the floor. Even that last day—with her hair, and then walking down the road—she barely tried to stop you. I think if it had been me I would have put up at least some kind of a fight."

When Josie stopped to take a breath, Celia remained perfectly still.

"Anyway, by the time I came around the curve, the car was already there. For a while I used to think that if I'd started running or if I'd yelled, things would have turned out different. It bothered me for a long time. But then I decided that I had to stop blaming myself, to stop blaming Djuna, to stop blaming my parents—and just try to accept what happened."

Perhaps if Celia made no sound, the silence would return them to where she thought they had been.

"Celie?" Josie asked. "You still there?"

"The piece I saw," Celia said. "At that Web site. Djuna had fallen and I was looking back at her as I ran away."

She closed her eyes, the way one does when making a wish.

"Well, that wasn't what I had in mind," Josie said, "but you're welcome to look at it that way if you want."

Celia lay down.

"The whole reason I make things with blank spaces," Josie continued, "is so that others can fill them in."

The absence of a car had allowed Celia to picture a forest. In a space empty save for three small figures, she had planted trees.

"Do you know that for a long time I was actually jealous?" Josie's voice was unceasing. "I mean, just because Becky and Leanne were farther down the road, they got to keep their lives. Their parents didn't send them to boarding school. For years afterward they didn't have nightmares. But I've accepted who it made me become. And to think that you're okay with what I've done . . ."

Celia got up from the bed and pressed her forehead to the window.

"Celie," Josie asked, "are you all right?"

Celia considered the question.

"No," she said. "I thought—"

She stopped. What she thought would make no difference.

CHAPTER 18

When he reached the car, Huck reflexively went for the right rear door. The front passenger seat had always belonged to Noreen. This disregard for the best use of leg room had pricked Huck's egalitarian sensibilities before he came to accept that until he and Celia exchanged formal vows, they would be relegated to the back like children in need of chaperones. Sliding into the front, Huck felt as if he had been promoted.

"Make yourself comfortable," Warren said. "There's a switch on the right-hand side that you can use to slide every-thing around. It's all electric, complete with heated seats. Some-times, when I open everything up to let the breeze in, I turn mine on. Go ahead and try it. It's like being in a fancy hotel and wrapping yourself in a prewarmed towel."

Huck pressed the switch. In minutes, the seat reached a temperature that reminded him of sitting in his own pee.

Before doing anything else, Warren reached for his driving gloves, which hung from the rearview mirror when not in use, dangling like a pair of sleeping bats. Donning them, Warren reminded Huck of a surgeon entering the operating theater: a man about to undertake a great responsibility; a man in love with his hands. With professional pride, he slid open the sunshade.

"I always wanted a convertible," Warren said. "But I never lived where it would be any kind of practical. When it's nice out, I'll slide open the moonroof and roll down all the windows, but only if I'm alone. Nor's kind of sensitive these days about her hair." When he pressed a switch, the moonroof raised itself at one end, half a drawbridge rising. Warren turned toward Huck, his eyebrows arched at a comparable angle.

"Cool," Huck said and Warren grinned, a boy with a Matchbox car.

"Now listen to this!" he said. Jazz ripped through the front seat. "Whoops!" he apologized, and readjusted the dial. "That's my solo driving volume. I'm actually happy when I hit a little traffic on my way to work. There are speakers in six different places!" As he pointed out each speaker's location, Huck realized they had never been without Celia's company. Warren released the parking brake, then paused and looked toward the house as if he had left something behind.

In the day's fading light, they passed cars in the final throes of the homeward commute. Huck saw pedestrians walking dogs inferior—as all others were—to the two he had left in Chicago. He suddenly longed for Bella spread out beside him on the couch, Sylvie at his feet as if his shoes were in need of protection. He wondered if these passing drivers and dog walkers would mistake him and Warren for father and son. Whenever they went out as a foursome, Huck was taken for Celia's husband. It was an assumption none of them ever corrected or used to segue into the obvious conversation, the one the four of them had never had.

Warren braked for a red light. "It's a quiet car," he said. "Handles well. Better than the rest of us, to tell the truth."

It took Huck a moment to realize what Warren meant.

"There's so little we can do for her anymore," he continued. "It's a funny complaint, I know. That's the way it's supposed to be, if you do your job right. She's a grown woman, but that doesn't mean that sometimes . . ." He shook his head. "Nor and I, we're both glad that she has you, especially now. Listen to this. Jazz Messengers. Birdland, 1954. Listen to the way Horace Silver keeps the rhythm."

When they reached the restaurant, Warren disappeared inside, returning minutes later with a large bag, accompanied by a young Japanese woman who smiled and nodded as he gestured emphatically in Huck's direction. Huck smiled and nodded in return before realizing that Warren was talking about the car. A moment later, the scent of new upholstery was overpowered by the tang of miso soup.

Huck was handed a bag the approximate weight of a toy poodle. He considered the possibility that he had only been invited along to prevent spillage.

"That was one of the owner's daughters," Warren explained. "Whenever you eat there, you see all the children and grandchildren around, helping out or playing in a corner. A real family business. Suki said they were looking to buy a new car. You know, sometimes I think I should have been an automobile salesman."

Huck held the bag on the floor between his feet. He talked about his classes, then fielded Warren's historical trivia questions. Eventually, Warren would revert to jazz or cars, but Huck had made his peace with this, had come to realize that as much as Warren liked people, they made him nervous, his congeniality constructed over a deep well of shyness. Huck suspected that Celia's preference for small-scale socializing was a more conventional strain of her father's anxiety, that nature rather than nurture was responsible for two people at ease in the company of data. Huck had witnessed Celia with a spreadsheet. There was relaxation in her concentration. She was like a beaver intent on building a dam, all native capacities put to best use. She had looked like that when she wrote poems but Huck had only seen that once, back when they were still in school and he had been falling in love.

It hadn't been any one thing. Love can't be mapped so easily, but Huck would have been dishonest not to count that stolen glimpse as a key moment, Celia sitting at her desk hunched over a sheet of paper, dancing with herself. She had written metered poems, a font of sestinas and villanelles in an age of blank verse. Then she had stopped, abandoning her poetry at graduation the way others renounced green hair or bisexuality. It had taken a while for Huck to decide that she had stopped completely, that she wasn't simply writing when alone. Even longer in coming had been the admission that there was nothing arty or visibly unusual about Celia, who wore business coordinates to work and flossed every night, even when that meant abandoning the narcotic afterglow of a good fuck. Huck wondered, if they were to meet now—but he wasn't sure how that would happen. His friends were teachers and musicians, hers were economists, social workers, and lawyers. On a Venn diagram, his circle and hers would not overlap. Were Huck today to come across Celia's Internet profile (he was infinitely grateful his bachelorhood had predated *that* quagmire), his eyes might stop only briefly to admire her face before moving on to more obvious quarry.

They were almost at the house when Warren turned to Huck as if they'd been speaking all along. "Tell me," he said. "She talks to you. Does she really think she did this thing?"

Huck pictured Celia in the guest bedroom watching for their return.

"She does," he said.

Warren shook his head. "I just don't understand it," he said. "This idea of hers . . . well, it's ridiculous. Forgive me, but there's really no other way to put it."

Huck could tell Warren didn't want to be looked at, but it was hard to keep facing front. Huck wondered if the confessional had bred in Warren a taste for sidelong confidence. When they reencountered a tree they had passed several minutes before, he realized that Warren had been circling the same few blocks, drumming his fingers on the wheel while working up the courage to begin.

"Cee Cee's a good person," Warren said. "She's sensitive, she's kind . . . practically all her life she's tried to help other people. I mean, sure, she can be stubborn sometimes, especially when she gets a certain idea in her head. But I hope that all this new business hasn't . . . that she hasn't . . . that you—"

"Warren, I'm in love with your daughter."

Warren let out a slow breath. "I suppose I already knew that. We love her too, of course. Which is why we were hoping you could help us to talk some sense into her. Encourage her to see reason. We can understand she might have a hard time taking it from us, but if it came from you . . ."

It was so unlike Warren to ask for anything that Huck didn't recognize at first that an appeal had been made. It *was* a quiet car. The rush of air into and over the narrow breach made by the moonroof was louder than the engine. He turned toward Warren, whose eyes darted away from the road just long enough for Huck to see the fear there.

"I'm not really comfortable with the idea of choosing sides," Huck said as mildly as he could. "I worry about saying something I'd regret later on."

Both Celia and her father draped their hands over the steering wheel at ten and two, as if resting them there rather than preventing a moving vehicle from crashing and bursting into flames.

"Did Cee Cee tell you that she talked to her mother?"

Huck nodded. "I remember her telling me that Noreen recalled things differently."

"Not differently," Warren amended. "Accurately. Let's suppose for the sake of argument that things happened the way Cee Cee says they did. Nor and I weren't with her at the time. A band of wild hyenas could have carried Djuna off. But Nor and I *were* around later, and I'm telling you that none of what happened afterward jibes with Cee Cee's version."

They stopped for a red light at an empty intersection.

"I'm not sure what you mean," Huck said, no longer certain he wanted Warren to be talking at all.

"Didn't she tell you?" Warren asked.

The light turned green. Warren drove around a squirrel. Huck couldn't tell if it was terrified or bored.

"Celia doesn't remember what happened afterward," he said. "She's tried, but she can't."

"Exactly," Warren confirmed. "If she did, she would have to see the illogic. Let's look at it from the beginning: Cee Cee says that she and Djuna were in the woods, that Djuna fell . . . into a hole or something, and that Cee Cee left her there. She was mad at Djuna; she made up the story about the car to get even, and once she realized what she had done, it felt too big to take back. Now, children sometimes do terrible things. I won't deny that, and I won't try to say that Cee Cee was an exception. But when children misbehave, especially when they misbehave as badly as Cee Cee is saying, what do they do after? They hide, that's what. If Cee Cee had done what she says she did, she would have never gone to Djuna's to tell Grace what had happened. I mean, it's one child in a million who might have the . . . I don't even know what you'd call it . . . the *gumption* to pull off a stunt like that. To lie like that, believably . . . and to Grace Pearson's face, no less. Not to mention to the police and to Nor and myself. That sort of thing takes practice. And Cee Cee was an honest kid. For crying out loud, look at her now! How much more straight an arrow can you get?"

Huck had discovered early in life that he was a good liar. True, it had started small, but he hadn't needed to practice. He had left his new jacket at the playground. When his mother asked where it was, he told her it had been taken from the class coat closet. Maybe he had an honest face, or maybe it was because he didn't look away, but his lies were never questioned. He had kept at it—his lies growing in scale, ambition, and frequency until he wasn't always sure what would happen when he opened his mouth—until he got so disgusted with himself that he gave it up cold turkey. It did not seem incredible to Huck that a person could succeed on a spectacularly grand scale her first time out, or that the experience might come to make honesty all the more appealing.

"This sounds like a conversation you should have with her," he said.

Warren nodded while looking ahead, as if agreeing with the angle of the windshield.

"Of course you're right," he said, "but you know how it is. In an ideal world I'm sure that she and I could talk about all of this . . . but the truth of the matter is that she's still my little girl. Perhaps it'll be different for you if you have a daughter, but for me . . . When it comes to Cee Cee, there are certain things. The search party, for instance. The day after Djuna disappeared, all the neighbors started organizing. My daughter's own best friend, and I didn't want to go. I know that sounds awful, but I couldn't imagine being the one to find something and having to go back home and tell her . . . having to watch her face—"

Warren's face went slack.

"But the point is," he continued, "I *did* search. We all did. We searched all along that road and beyond and we didn't find a single thing. Not a shoe. Not a hair ribbon. So you can understand that when Cee Cee says she left Djuna back there, I find it just a little hard to believe."

At some point Warren must have changed course without Huck realizing it, because they were pulling up to the house. The steep grade of the driveway was custom-made for sleds and tricycles, a slant that signaled a dozing child to either awaken or feign deeper sleep in order to be carried inside.

"Well, here we are," Warren said. "Why don't you grab the takeout. I bet you a nickel Nor put out these square plates she got on sale a couple months ago, supposed to be specially made for eating Asian food." He chuckled. "As if the shape of the plate would make a difference."

Warren climbed out and strode the length of the front walk. As he reached the house, he froze for a moment before removing his driving gloves, then looked back at the car before thrusting them into his pants, his pockets bulging as he went inside.

CHAPTER 19

Noreen had put out the square plates, had even brewed green tea for the sake of authenticity, the steaming cups sipped in ceremoniously minute quantities to mitigate the repercussions of dinnertime caffeine. Devoid of appetite, Celia reflexively shuttled a piece of eel and cucumber roll beneath the table. Homesickness was not the proper term for the dog-shaped void that met her outstretched fingers. She did not know what to call it, this desire to return not just to another place but to another time.

"How did your phone call go, sweetie?" Noreen asked. "Did you . . . Was it Mrs. Pearson?"

Celia shook her head. Since her silent arrival to the table,

Huck's stare had slowly escalated to the one he beamed across restaurants to hail preoccupied servers. Were Celia in Chicago, she'd be talking, or at least working up to it, but her parents' house annulled the habits she and Huck had built over ten years.

"You look so upset," Noreen coaxed, "and I've been worried all this time that if you *did* end up talking to Djuna's mother, she might, well . . . I don't know quite how to say this without sounding awful, but . . . I didn't *like* them, Celia. I never did."

For the first time since dinner had begun, Huck's attention shifted. Celia felt her jaw unclench.

"Who?" she asked.

Noreen took a breath. "I can't tell you what a relief it is to finally say this. Ask your father. When you were little it took all my self-control to hold myself back. I'm sorry, sweetie, but I never liked Djuna or her mother."

Celia looked to Warren, uncertain what she'd heard.

Her father nodded. "Back then," he said, "at night, after you'd gone to bed, your mother and I would stay up talking about it."

"They weren't nice people," Noreen explained. "It wasn't Djuna's fault, of course. She was only following the examples she'd been given. I blame Grace—"

"And the husband," Warren said.

"Who knows?" said Noreen. "Dennis was so rarely there. All those academic conferences. I heard that he exhausted the math department's budget, that he had to pay for trips out of his own pocket. And who could blame him, with someone like Grace waiting for him at home?"

"How can you say that? Mrs. Pearson was totally great!" Celia said, surprised at the ferocity and paucity of her defense. As far as she could remember, the last *totally great* thing in her life had been a Genesis album.

"She adored you," Noreen agreed. "And I could see how much you adored her right back. It was impossible to compete. Here was a woman who had traveled, who had this beautifully furnished home, who had opinions about art and food—"

"About everything, really—" Warren interjected.

"—and if you didn't agree with her . . . or worse, didn't have an opinion of your own . . . about Victorian architecture, for example, or modernist poetry—"

"She was a poet?" Huck asked.

"An English professor," Celia said. "She loved my poems."

"Djuna's mother loved everything Celie did," Noreen said. "She took her under her wing. But as for everyone else . . ."

Warren shook his head. "Notwithstanding how she treated Cee Cee, she was a snob, plain and simple. Noreen and I are not unintelligent people and she made us feel like rubes. She enjoyed it."

Celia appealed to Huck. "She wasn't like that! I learned so much just by listening to her. She was the first adult not to talk *down* to me. She never treated me like a child."

"But you *were* a child," Noreen reminded her. "You were eleven years old. We didn't know what to do. We knew we couldn't try to keep you from seeing Djuna. So we decided to let things run their course."

"Wait it out," Warren said.

"Celie and Djuna were so . . . mercurial," Noreen explained. "We thought if we were patient, the friendship would burn itself out. Or at least fade into something a little less . . ."

"Extreme," Warren suggested.

Noreen nodded. "But in the meantime, we saw Celie becoming more like her . . . less tolerant, less considerate, more willing to make a joke at someone else's expense."

"We didn't turn a blind eye," Warren said. "When she was at home, we expected her to behave."

"But it was awful, watching her change like that, knowing that we had to let her make her own decisions about who she wanted to spend time with, who she wanted to be."

"All *we* could do," Warren told Huck, "was hope that we were right about the person we felt she was at heart."

Celia tried to content herself with the backs of her parents' heads. She was certain that without Huck to address, her parents would not have been able to speak at all.

"And then," Noreen told Huck, "all our worries were taken away. And as ashamed as I am to say it, I was relieved."

When Noreen turned toward Celia, her face reflected a fear that Celia had thought was hers alone.

"I didn't think I would ever tell you that," Noreen said. "I was sure you'd hate me for it. It's a mother's job to show her best self to her children. But you're grown now, and it's something I still think about."

For a moment, they were the only two people in the room.

"Your mother is being too hard on herself," Warren said. "She was heartbroken for Djuna, and for Djuna's mother, for all that poor woman went through."

"No parent deserves that," Noreen confirmed. "It was shameful, really, the way the community turned its back on Grace." She shook her head. "The way I turned *my* back."

"It's okay, Nor. Water under the bridge," Warren said, but his wife was contemplating their daughter.

"She called once," Noreen said. "It was maybe a week after Djuna was gone. I came home to her message on the machine. It was the first time I'd ever heard Grace sounding anything less than completely self-assured."

"Who was she calling for?" Celia whispered.

"She said she was calling for me," Noreen said, "but it was you she asked about. She wanted to know how you were doing, if you were eating and sleeping all right. I never called back."

As the sky outside the window darkened, the sodium street-lights flickered on. Once, there'd been a propane gas lamp at the foot of every driveway, a glowing yellow trail leading home.

"How long did they stay?" Celia asked.

"Who?" Noreen asked.

"Djuna's parents," Celia said. "How long after did they stay in the house?"

Noreen shook her head. "Six months? Nine months, maybe? If it's something you need to know, I can—"

"I was just wondering," Celia said. "When I drove past, the colors were gone."

"The house has been that way for a long time," Noreen said. "After Grace left—"

"She's listed," Celia said. "I found her straight off, but I wanted to reach the others first. I wanted to be able to tell Mrs. Pearson that I'd told everyone the truth. Except that when I talked to Becky and Josie, when I told them what had really happened, they both said that they remembered seeing a car."

"You mean that they—" Noreen began.

"They don't believe me either," Celia said. She tried to ignore the sight of three faces going slack with relief.

Warren leaned forward, and for once Celia found herself looking forward to one of his nervous non sequiturs about cars or music, started counting the seconds until she might excuse herself from the table without seeming rude.

"It's strange what people do or don't remember," he said instead. "Once, I asked Jem if he recalled that last day in his room." He paused. "You and I have never talked about this, Cee Cee. I always meant to tell you, but it never seemed like the right time."

When he looked to his wife, Noreen nodded, and something inside Celia's father unfurled.

"Your brother told me he remembered watching himself on the floor," Warren said. "An out-of-body experience, I guess you'd call it, which was something he'd never had before. He said he kind of liked it, but he could tell that something was wrong because he couldn't feel anything. It wasn't like being numb. It was like he didn't have anything to do with the person he was looking at. He remembered wondering if he was dying, if maybe he was already dead. Then he heard a voice calling his name, and that was when the griffin came into his room. Jem said it was as big as a man, with gold wings and a golden tail. At first he was scared because he thought maybe it meant he really was dead. But then he felt himself being lifted, and he wasn't on the floor anymore. And then . . ." Warren gazed at his lap. His shoulders shuddered and he took a few deep breaths. "And then," he continued, "he told me that he loved me, but in his mind it would always be a griffin that had saved him. I told him I didn't care what he saw walk into his room that day. All that I wanted was for him to be all right."

Noreen reached across the table, and Warren met her there, his arm longer than hers, their hands joining just short of center.

"Cee Cee," he said, "I can't bring myself to believe that you left Djuna in those woods, but even if it were true, I'd love you all the same."

"You'll always be our little girl," Noreen whispered.

Within minutes, the remains of the take-out dinner would be eaten. Noreen would shoo Huck from the dirty dishes, but allow Celia to spell her at the sink. Warren would spin his newest vinyl acquisition and defend the superior playback qualities of the Stereohedron stylus. Celia would have to remind herself that the conversation had happened at all.

- - - - - - - - -

Once Warren and Noreen had retreated upstairs, Celia and Huck settled in front of the television. When Huck left the den, Celia assumed he'd gone to the bathroom until his absence stretched long.

"Front or back?" she asked when he reappeared.

"Back, of course. A seven-foot privacy fence is a beautiful thing."

She wanted to tell him not to sit back down, worried about the smell seeding itself into the couch.

"I thought you didn't do that here," she said.

"Extenuating circumstances." His arm, still cold from the outside air, chilled the skin at the back of her neck.

Celia feigned interest in the TV. "Just hold off tomorrow, okay? At least while Jeremy's around."

Huck rolled his eyes. "Jeez, Ceel, I've never been anything but completely conscientious." He chuckled. "Though your brother totally knows."

"How?" she asked. "You haven't done it in front—"

"Oh, come on," Huck groaned. "We talked about it once, that's all. He said that smoking was one of the things he missed the least. Said it always made him feel stupid and slightly paranoid." He smiled. "Man, how about your dad tonight? Just when I think he's all old jazz and manual transmissions, he goes and says something like that."

"Yeah," Celia said. Her voice rose to her ear like windborne ash. "Jem loved griffins. He went through this whole mythological phase starting from when he was, like, ten and going until he was at least thirteen." She sighed. "I wish you hadn't smoked."

"Ceel," he said. "Is that really what you want to be talking about?"

"It's why you can't get up on time anymore," she said. "It's why you've been going straight to sleep when the movie ends instead of . . ." She stared at the television. "You've been unhappy for a long time."

Huck exhaled a long breath.

"I know," he said.

"It's like you start shutting down and you don't even know that you're doing it. You start coming up with ways not to have to deal with me . . . volunteering for after-school stuff, deciding that you need to watch every film with a certain actress."

"I wish it had all been as clear to me," he said.

She shook her head. "I knew that I needed to say something, but if I told you, then we'd have to deal with it, and if we dealt with it, that might mean . . ." She tried to concentrate on the sound of her breath. "So instead, I just tried to live with it, until one morning I was on my way to work . . . and now, here I am."

"That's good, Ceel. What's happening here is a good thing."

"But what's the point if no one believes me?"

"This isn't about belief," Huck said.

"Sure it is."

"It's not," Huck said. "No one thinks that you're lying, Ceel. They just don't agree with what you remember."

"Including you," Celia said.

Huck shook his head. "It doesn't matter what I think."

"Actually, it does."

The television was unloading the tail end of a cable movie.

The timed lamps downstairs had switched off, leaving the two of them pallid in the television's sloughed light.

"Okay then." Huck sighed. "If you really want to know, I think considering that Becky, and Josie, and your parents—"

"Wait." She turned away. "I changed my mind."

They stared at the television.

"I'm going to see Leanne first thing in the morning," Celia said.

Huck pressed the remote's red button. It became very quiet. "I think that's a really bad idea," he said.

"It might be," she agreed, "but I'm going to do it anyway. In case this is my only chance."

"This isn't the same as your job, Ceel. You don't get special access to all the places you need in order to fulfill your fact-finding mission. You are distinctly uninvited."

"It's okay," Celia said. "I won't ask you to go with me."

She closed her eyes.

"When we get back to Chicago," he said, "I think you should start seeing a therapist."

She remained perfectly still. She could hear her pulse in her ear.

"You too," she said. They sat in sodium-tinted darkness, the room suffused in an orange glow. When a car passed, the beam of its headlamps cast itself like a searchlight across the room's surfaces, an illuminated parade of shapes in brief rally against the night.

CHAPTER 20

Celia left the next morning while Huck was still sleeping. She told her parents she had a breakfast date, which was true enough to get her to the car guilt-free. She would have been terrible company, refusing coffee and unable to eat. Celia felt better in the car, but then saw she'd need to waste at least forty-five minutes before it became a civilized hour to stop by. Leanne's address put her in Pritchard. Celia had only ever been there once before, to visit a flea market with Huck, the two of them treading between rickety folding tables heaped with ceremonial swords, homemade deer jerky, 9/11 memorial T-shirts, animal-shaped bottle openers, and secondhand children's clothing, a pageant they'd fled after fifteen minutes.

Leanne lived a few miles east of the flea market, in a neighborhood of small, one-story homes just past a trailer park and a gas station that advertised tune-ups and live bait. Celia drove past kids on battered bicycles, a man leaning over the hood of a car, a girl sitting on her front stoop chewing the hair of a Barbie doll. Leanne's was the nicest house on her block, with a trimmed lawn, a recent paint job, and a sturdy porch sheltering a wicker chair in good repair. Celia drove past once without stopping, then circled around and pulled into the driveway. She parked behind an aging pickup truck with a Wilson-Smith University decal in its back window and a bumper sticker that read NONE OF YOUR BUSINESS.

She slammed the car door, hoping the sound might carry through the open windows. The porch steps creaked under her weight. Flanking the wicker chair was a wicker side table that held a full ashtray and a stack of magazines. Celia tried to create an adult portrait of Leanne sitting in that chair, reading a magazine and smoking a cigarette, but all she could see was a skinny girl with crooked ash-blond bangs and ragged fingernails. Celia stood on the porch a moment, hoping it would be enough: just the outer screen door was closed. "Hello?" she called. When nothing happened, she crossed to the door and placed her face against the mesh. She made out a stairwell and an easy chair. From the back of the house, a shadow ambled forward.

"Can I help you?" a man asked from the other side of the screen. Celia couldn't tell whether she looked as familiar to him as he looked to her.

"Hi," she began. "I'm an old friend of Leanne's and I just

happened to be in the neighborhood." She gasped inwardly at the flimsiness of the lie. "Did I manage to catch her at home?"

The man looked her over.

"No, you did not," he finally answered.

He stepped onto the porch. He was slender with a gentle face, the type Celia would have had a crush on, but when she ran through her mental teenage roster of heartbreaks and unrequited loves, she came up blank. She tried and failed to place him in the middle school cafeteria or a high school classroom. When he looked her over a second time, she realized they were playing the same memory game. He gave a small grunt.

"I know who you are," he said.

"You do?"

"You're Celia Durst."

"Have we met?" she asked.

"Not really," he said.

"Because you look familiar to me too. Are you and Leanne related?"

"You got it in one," he said.

"Well, it's nice to meet you," she said, and held out her hand. He hesitated before offering his. "I can't tell if I'm remembering you because we met as kids or because you've got your sister's eyes."

"It's the resemblance," he said. "We've also got the same sense of humor."

Down the block a screen door slammed and Celia turned toward the sound. A dog bounded from a house, dragging a boy by its leash. When Celia turned back toward Leanne's brother, his wariness seemed to have been replaced by something milder.

"You back visiting your folks or something?" he asked.

She nodded. "I forgot how nice it was here in spring."

"It can get real pretty."

"Are you visiting too?"

When he laughed, Celia could see his sister in his smile.

"Me?" he said. "No. I'm more or less stuck with this place."

"What about Leanne?"

He shook his head. "Lee's the same as me."

"Were you a grade or two above us? Maybe we saw each other on the playground?"

"We didn't."

"But still," she persisted, "it's not like Jensenville's a huge place. We must have—"

"Look," he said. "I know you've been sending e-mails and I also know you've come here uninvited, so I'm not going to ask you in, but since you're here anyway I guess I don't mind talking with you on the porch. You want something? I've got water."

"Do you think Leanne will be back soon?"

He shook his head. "Don't count on it."

"Water's fine," she said, and he disappeared back through the door into the darkened house.

She sat in the single chair. Someone across the street was blaring rap through an open window, the bass ricocheting against the side of the neighboring house. She knew Leanne's brother had returned by the slam of the screen door behind her.

"You comfortable?" he asked, and she realized she was meant to turn her chair to face him. He was standing behind a second wicker chair that he had brought from inside and still gripped in his hands. A single glass of water rested on the table beside her.

"Sure," she said.

"You're sitting in a chair that Lee restored. Sturdied up the frame and recaned the whole thing. You should have seen it before—the seat had a big hole busted in it and the entire piece had been painted this trashy shade of orange. Stripping the paint off was a bitch, but it sure looks beautiful now."

"Sounds like a pretty big job."

"It was, but that was just what Lee needed. Wicker restoration is what got Lee through the first few years of recovery. Now it's kind of a vocation." He pointed to a sign in the front window that read WICKER BY LEE—RESTORATION AND ORIGINAL CREATIONS in bold blue type. "Pretty much everybody's got an old busted wicker chair lying around," he continued. "It's good furniture and it lasts a lifetime if you treat it right. I bet your folks have a chair or two that Lee could fix for them."

"Um, I don't know. I'll have to check." She reached for the water and took a sip. It was warm.

"Now that is something Lee would surely appreciate," he said. "Remind me and I'll give you a business card before you go." He looked at her. She feigned absorption in her glass.

"I'm glad to know Leanne is doing well," she said. Her chair creaked every time she moved.

"Yeah," he said. "There were some real rough times. Really tough. Anybody who at all gave a shit for Lee was pretty worried, but now Lee is doing all right." He nodded. "You went to college," he told her. "What did you study?"

"I ended up as an economics major."

"An economist? Now that actually sounds useful. One thing I could never understand was people paying all that money to study English or religion or whatnot. You must be doing pretty well for yourself over in Chicago."

"How did you know I was—"

"Your e-mails," he said.

"But I didn't—"

"You're not the only one who knows how to type a name into the Internet."

He leaned against the house as he looked her over, his eyes studying her as if he could see through to her veins.

"You know," he said, "Lee was kind of freaked when you turned up again after all these years."

"Well, I really appreciate her writing me back."

"You were somebody Lee had been pretty happy to leave behind," he said. "It's actually fairly fucked up, you sitting here on Lee's porch, acting like this perfectly considerate person."

"I was hoping to apologize," she said.

"You already did."

Celia shook her head. "Not really. Not in the way she deserves."

"But Lee didn't want that," he said, his shaking head mocking her own. "Lee wanted never to see you again, so what does that do to your apology? It turns it into more harm done, doesn't it? Some new messed-up thing that you've got to make amends for."

Celia could not stop staring.

"I'm sorry," she said.

"Leanne was so unhappy," he continued. "She didn't need any help from you and Djuna on that account. Ever since she could remember, she knew she was different. She was already the most miserable little girl, and then the two of you took that and cranked it up higher than it should have been possible to go."

Celia stared, and he smiled, neither of them able to stop.

"I hated you for what you did," he said, those words from between his smiling lips raising the hair on the back of Celia's neck. "I thought I'd gotten past that, but seeing you like this, I realize that I still do."

"You and Leanne must be pretty close," she said.

"As close as it's possible to be in this world."

"It was wrong of me to come." Celia shook her head. "I don't expect you to believe it, but I'm not usually this . . . I should be going." She began to stand.

"Not yet," he said in a way that froze her where she was.

The music from across the street had stopped. It was quiet save for the distant sounds of cars.

"What time did you used to wake up for school?" he asked.

"Excuse me?"

"I said, what time?"

She looked at him.

"It's not a trick question," he said, leaning closer. "Back when you were still just an innocent little girl, what time did you wake up to get ready for school?"

He was wearing a T-shirt and she could tell that he liked to work out. His arms bulged from shoulder to forearm before tapering into slim, almost dainty wrists. If she had stood, her mouth would have just grazed the top of his head, but he had more muscle. She considered returning to the car. Instead, she stayed where she was and looked at him looking at her, his question spiking the air between them.

"Seven o'clock?" she offered. "Seven thirty? I'm sorry, I really don't—"

"Every morning Leanne woke up at five A.M.," he said. "Five A.M. to prepare for your stupid inspections. She'd stand in front of the mirror, looking at her hair, her clothes, her personality for chrissake, wondering what she could do to get a passing grade. And you were so clever about it. You let her pass just often enough not to allow her to give up hope, to let her think there was some sort of objective logic. That the two of you actually *could* help her to become a better girl."

Celia remembered making up the form with Djuna each morning on the bus, drawing boxes with a black pen in a notebook placed between them. Half the time they would fill in the grades before they even got to school, in order to get it out of the way.

"I'm ashamed of what we did," she said softly. "It was stupid and mean and I wish I could say that I wasn't aware of that at the time, but I'm sure that I was. I do know that we didn't do it according to any sort of thought-out plan."

"Well, I guess that makes you born geniuses of the mind-fuck," he said. "Must feel good to be so naturally gifted at something. Leanne sure as hell wasn't. Not at the most basic little thing. You had her so whipped, she actually felt relieved that day you told her you were going to leave her in the woods. There wasn't even any need for you to have walked her there. After that haircut, she was so far gone that you could have pointed in any direction you wanted and told her to walk until she fell off the edge of the world."

"Was that what we were doing that day?" Celia asked softly.

He laughed. "It was *your* brilliant plan, only by the time we started out you weren't so sure you liked it anymore. In some corner of your puny little heart you thought it might be *wrong* to leave someone in the woods like that. But by then, of course, it was too late because Djuna thought it was the best idea she'd ever heard."

The chair he had brought for himself was like Celia's, but smaller—the sort of chair that might be used at a writing desk. He was still standing behind it, sometimes grasping the top rail with one hand. Every time he did, the wicker creaked like old bones.

"Final question," he continued. "When was the first time Leanne tried to kill herself?"

Celia swallowed her breath.

"Tell me," he said, his voice louder. "Because I'm really curious. Do you know the first time Leanne tried to take her own life?"

"No," she whispered.

"No," he repeated. "No, you do not."

He drew a lighter and a pack of Marlboros from his shirt

pocket, tapped a cigarette into his palm and lit it, gazing at the street. Exhaled smoke wafted past the porch and into the yard. A newer, nicer pickup than the one in Leanne's driveway cruised by.

"It was the summer after fifth grade," he said. "July 1986. She tried to swallow a bottle of aspirin, but threw it up halfway and passed out. I suppose it was a good thing it happened in that order and not the other way around. As it was, she cleaned up the mess when she woke up and no one was the wiser. She never told a soul."

Celia opened her mouth, then closed it again.

"All through that whole school year, she'd prayed for the two of you to be punished," he said. "Every night before bed she got on her knees and asked for something terrible to happen. Then it did. What do you do when your prayers get answered like that?"

"I'm so sorry," Celia murmured.

"Well thank you," he said. "Thank you, Celia Durst, for being sorry."

Celia thought back to the birthday party, to the small living room, to the photos of two girls, sisters for a hairsbreadth of time.

"You—" she began. She couldn't look at him the same way, and this shamed her—one last, unredeemable offense.

He started toward her and she braced herself against the chair. He stood over her and looked down. The eyes were exactly the same.

"I owe you *nothing*," Lee hissed. "You aren't family and you sure as hell are not my friend. You, Celia Durst, are only one of the many, many things in my life that I have left behind."

He stubbed his cigarette in the ashtray beside Celia, turned back around, and returned to the front door.

"You found your way out here okay so I won't give you directions on how to get back," he said. He pulled the door open. "But I will say this: if you want to do me a good turn, I highly suggest that for the rest of this natural-born life you keep away. And in the next life, when you come back as a bug or as a vermin, you'd best keep a healthy distance between yourself and the sole of my shoe. Now leave here and don't come back."

The screen door closed behind him. Celia heard Lee's footsteps inside the house, and then she heard nothing at all.

CHAPTER *21*

Huck shifted into Celia's space on the mattress. His sleep had been punctuated by dream arguments that left him exhausted when the bed had creaked its alarm that morning. By the time he'd said, "C'mere," Celia was already half dressed. She'd returned to him just long enough to kiss his forehead.

Huck wished this friend of hers could have fled farther than the neighboring town, somewhere beyond the operational radius of Celia's desire. He had never thought he'd find a downside to Celia's determination, but here it was. Her insistence that good could come of her visit to Leanne was no different, in his mind, than believing in fairies. Such unyielding persistence was the closest Celia came to the bully she claimed to have once been.

Warren and Noreen, earlier risers both, would already be waiting with fresh coffee. Huck could picture Warren at the stove minding a pan of eggs while Noreen sliced fruit, Saturday's ritual breakfast. In the early years there had been bacon, until Warren had started monitoring his cholesterol. Its disappearance had coincided with Huck's own first concessions to age—the stretching needed before and after a pickup basketball game, the supreme importance of getting to bed no later than ten thirty on a school night—measures that had revoked any lingering belief in his immortal youth. Around the same time that Huck conceded his afternoon candy bar to a slowing metabolism, he had attended a three-day teaching conference in Wisconsin where he met a teacher from North Dakota—a state he was in no danger of ever visiting—who had the most beautifully unruly hair and an adorable history teacher's crush on Alexander Hamilton. It would have been perfectly safe; they didn't even know each other's last names. The final night of the conference, Huck had paced his hotel room pondering the ways in which a one-night stand might impact all his nights to come. In the end he had called Celia, ascended into telephonic perversity, and fallen asleep a happy man.

Huck stepped into yesterday's pants and slipped on a fresh shirt, debating whether to go online now, or after appearing downstairs. He decided it was less rude to delay than to disappear once he had come down, but he would need to be careful. If he arrived too late, the fruit salad would be portioned into individual bowls and wrapped in plastic. Noreen and

Warren would be sipping coffee before empty, waiting plates, their apparent happiness at the timing of Huck's appearance belied by the dryness of the eggs.

Huck crept down the hall to prolong the impression he was still in bed. Entering Jeremy's old room felt like a violation of their tacit friendship. Nine Christmases ago, when Celia's brother had been attending community college and daily NA meetings, Jeremy and Huck had each recognized in the other a fellow survivor of a chancy adolescence. Huck knew he had been spared Jeremy's battles only due to the random calibration of his endorphin receptors and plain, dumb luck. Having scaled and descended different cliff faces seemed less important than their both having returned alive.

As Huck waited for the computer to boot, he spotted two familiar books on an abandoned bookshelf, a fistful of multi-sided dice gathering dust beside them. The mounted cavalier on the cover of Jeremy's old *D&D Player's Handbook* was as familiar to Huck as his own face, the griffin on the *Monster Manual* an old friend. Huck blew dust from the dice and remembered when resting them in his palm had felt like holding precious gems. When he returned his attention to the computer, he felt like he'd been welcomed.

Huck hadn't expected so many images at the art gallery's Web site, and had begun to worry he'd somehow missed the ones Celia was talking about, when there they were. Jocelyn Linke's figures were suggestive of bodies rather than imitative: they did not always have the right number of fingers; some of them had extra hands, or peepholes installed in their torsos. The realism of the girls' faces jarred with their bodies, their heads more precise than anything below the neck. The first piece showed four girls walking in formation around a fifth, whose arms were crossed as if tied. In the second, two girls argued with a vehemence that could have been funny if their faces hadn't looked so grim. One of these girls echoed one of Celia's studio portraits on the family picture wall—chin-length hair tucked behind the ears, nose just beginning to elongate to its final, regal length—but the exaggerated ferocity of the features turned the face into a weapon.

In the last image, a girl with a dark ponytail sat apart from two others, one of them Celia, her face crossed by a grief that reminded Huck of that famous painting by Munch, expressing the sort of deep emotion sighted only rarely, like some terrible comet, at moments of greatest loss. It made Huck wish he had been there. Never mind that he would have been ten and living in Cleveland, over a decade removed from his and Celia's first meeting. He envied what Josie had seen. The shame of this did not lessen his want, and the realization that he might eventually get his wish briefly eclipsed the fact that it would come at Celia's expense. As long as they were still together when life's built-in schedule of loss inflicted such grief on Celia again, Huck would fulfill this basest urge to own every aspect of his lover.

Huck turned off the computer. He was exactly on time— at the stairwell he heard Noreen setting out the breakfast things. He would peaceably submit to her proxy mothering and Warren's music soliloquies. Coming to terms with his putative in-laws had been like making peace with his parents, only more efficient: compressed into the span of a few Christ-

mases and entirely without their knowledge, Huck had tra-
versed unquestioning approval and reflexive rejection to arrive
at acceptance. The experience had reinforced his notion that
adulthood didn't change people so much as smooth their edges,
but now he wondered if there wasn't a chrysalis model of
maturity. Perhaps the child transformed itself into an entirely
different organism, its remnants discarded with the ruptured
cocoon. Huck wondered if the Celia he knew was recogniza-
ble to friends who had only known her earlier incarnation, or
if they were as baffled by her now as he was by the girl she
claimed to have once been.

CHAPTER *22*

Lee's voice echoed in Celia's head on the drive back from Pritchard. Celia replayed his appearance at the door, his handing her a drink, his enumeration of all that she'd forgotten along with all that she had no right to know. Each of Celia's mistakes sat inside her like a swallowed stone.

She arrived home to Jeremy's car in the driveway. By the time she'd come up the walk, her father was standing just inside the front door.

"Here she is!" he announced to Daniel squirming in his arms. "Here's Aunt Cee Cee."

"No," Daniel pronounced and angled toward her, his lips a wet pucker, his face speckled with crumbs.

Celia leaned to meet her nephew's mouth.

"Hello, Daniel," she said. As his proto-kiss grazed her cheek, Jeremy and Huck emerged from the hallway.

"Hey, Cee," Jeremy said. His hug smelled like baby powder. "I see you've met Dr. No."

"No," Daniel said, and reached for his father.

People took Celia and Jeremy for brother and sister only in the company of their parents, whose salient qualities had been divvied up neatly between them. Jeremy had his father's black hair and chestnut eyes, but those eyes were close-set like Noreen's, his features distributed more centrally than Celia's, as if someone hadn't been sure his face had the room. They were both tall but where Celia was lanky, Jeremy was the kind of person you'd want beside you in a stiff wind or while leaping from rock to rock. Celia blamed recovery and marriage equally for her brother's transformation from solid to chunky. His face, neck, and belly had thickened, and she suspected a stranger would take him for the older sibling now. The thought distressed her more than it appealed to her vanity, though she didn't think Jeremy would mind. Marriage and fatherhood had buoyed him into an almost continuous state of gratitude that Celia would have found irritating in anyone who was not family, or for whom it had not been so hard-earned.

"It's great to see you," he told her. He balanced Daniel on his hip with an ease Celia had previously assigned to mothers. "Pam is in the den," he said, "being waited on by Mom hand and foot."

"Congratulations," Celia said.

He smiled. "We weren't expecting it, but we weren't exactly surprised either."

"How's Pam feeling?"

"Oh, she'll be happy to tell you all about it," Jeremy said.

Daniel pumped his legs.

"What is it, bugaloo? You wanna walk?" Jeremy grinned. "He's like one of those wind-up toys," he told her as he released Daniel and shadowed him down the hall.

"How are you?" Huck asked under his breath as they headed toward the den.

Celia felt her legs wobble, wished she could pull Huck by the hand to some quiet corner of the house and tell him everything. "You were right," she said. "I shouldn't have gone."

"What's that?" Warren called.

"Nothing, Daddy."

"Did you see your friend?" her father asked.

Celia paused, unsure how to answer. The timeline that began with Leanne and ended with Lee wasn't Celia's to draw. To spin her own thread connecting the girl in faded hand-me-downs to the man who had spat Celia's name would just be more trespassing, a violation of the distance she'd been warned to keep.

"She wasn't there," Celia said, and followed the rest of them in.

Pam waved at Celia from Noreen's recliner. "Pardon me for not getting up," she said, "but Mom installed me in here so good I don't think I could get out without a trailer hitch." Pam looked big for thirteen weeks and Celia wondered if it had to do with the shirt. She suspected most maternity clothing of being constructed to exaggerate the condition of its wearer, wordlessly accomplishing the mission of T-shirts that read BUN IN THE OVEN or BAKING MY LITTLE BEAN, an entire industry predicated on the pregnant woman's fear of being taken for fat. Celia had hoped a natural affinity would develop between herself and her brother's wife, but after four Christmases Pam still addressed Celia with impenetrable cheer. Pam belonged to a Tompkins County strain of brothers, sisters, uncles, aunts, and cousins who never crossed state lines. Celia could tell Pam liked her, but restraint seemed to run in Pam's blood, an innate animal caution toward a creature that had left the forest.

"How do you feel?" she asked, and Pam made a face.

"I won't bore you with it," Pam said, "but let's just say I'm on the baked potato and banana diet."

"I have both of those," Noreen trilled from the kitchen. "I had a feeling you might not be interested in quiche."

Pam blanched. "Please don't mention anything having to do with eggs," she whispered.

The next half hour was devoted to observing Daniel's circumnavigation of the first floor, sometimes waving like royalty, sometimes dragging a plush lobster the size of his torso. Over brunch, Pam's tales of morning sickness chorused each ode to infancy—what Daniel could say, what he could eat, how he slept, how many teeth he had. The monomania of first-time parents and grandparents afforded Celia refuge behind grins and nods, though Huck wasn't fooled.

At the meal's end, Warren enlisted Huck's help in the kitchen while Noreen disappeared with Pam and Daniel into the den, leaving Celia alone with her brother.

"Don't get mad," Jeremy told her after the room's evacuation, "but Mom and Dad told me why you're here." Celia longed for some of the ease in Jeremy's voice, the legacy of daily conversations with their parents that she would never share.

"That's all right," she said. "I should have told you when you called."

They sat in the chairs that had always been theirs. It was possible they had not been alone in a room since the Clinton administration. The skin around Jeremy's eyes was cross-hatched with tiny lines, as if he'd spent his life in the sun rather than in the ninth-cloudiest city in America.

"Jem," she said. "What was I like back then?"

Her brother swirled a water glass in his hands, his eyes fixed on the small whirlpool inside.

"Which 'back then'?" he asked.

"When we were kids," she said. "Did I pick on you?" She had given up on *little* long ago, but *younger* was equally irrelevant. The man sitting across the table from her was simply her brother.

"I'd like to know what you remember," she said.

Jeremy appraised her from across the table. "You want me to list all the terrible things you did to me when we were little?"

She nodded.

"All right, let me think." He made his mental tally. "Okay," he said. "For years when we played Monopoly, you got me to trade you things like Park Place for Baltic Avenue by telling me that purple was a better color than blue. Once, you handed me water mixed with toothpaste and a few drops of liquid soap and told me it was a new kind of milk. And sometimes you'd hide behind the couch and wait until I came in so you could growl like a wolf and scare the bejesus out of me." He leaned back in his chair.

"Is that everything?" she asked.

He nodded. "That's it. All the biggest stuff, anyway. According to Mom, you bit my finger right after I came home from the hospital to see if I was a real baby, but even my memory doesn't go back that far."

She gave a shaky exhale.

"Cee?" he asked. "You okay? I'm not holding out on you. Really, you were a good big sister."

"Even when Djuna was around?"

He shrugged. "You were meaner then, but we had fun."

"How was I mean?" she whispered.

"Just stupid stuff. You'd call me names sometimes, or if the three of us were playing together I always had to be the slave or the dog or the baby. But, man, you two were entertaining. You were so intense about everything. My friends and I were never like that. I mean, sure, sometimes we'd fight over who got to be Boba Fett, but then we'd tackle each other and we'd be over it. Pam says it's a girl thing." He smiled. "I have to say, as much as I love women, looking at what Pam's going through now and what you went through back then, I don't envy any of you one bit."

From the den they could hear their mother crooning tuneless nursery rhymes.

"Jem?" Celia said. "Back when we were kids, there was this girl. The one you said you didn't remember on the phone."

"Leanne?"

Celia nodded. "She was this tomboy from the east side who kind of adopted us one day. Started eating at our lunch table, following us around at recess, would pretty much do anything we told her."

"There are always kids like that," Jeremy said.

"I guess, but we took it too far. Leanne wanted to be like us, and it became this game. Every day Djuna and I would rate her, and whenever she scored too low . . ."

"What?"

"It's not even like I forgot," Celia said softly. "I just sort of glossed over it. Jem, we were terrible. We invented all these 'treatments' that we said would help her, like only eating carrots or using lotion instead of shampoo. And whenever she failed our inspections we'd do stupid stuff like call her Reject or tell her that she could only talk if one of us talked to her first. She'd always do it. And because we were 'good girls,' and Leanne didn't tell, no one ever knew."

"How long?" he asked.

"A while. All winter and into the spring. We did it every day. We never got bored. But she must have, because finally . . . I didn't remember this part until I talked to Josie."

"Cee?" Jeremy asked. "You okay?"

"No. I'm just so . . . I can't even look at you right now."

"You don't have to tell me."

Celia nodded. "I do. This one day, Leanne showed up wearing all the wrong things . . . brown pants and a soccer shirt, black sneakers, and even a cowboy belt. We always rated her in three categories: colors, fashion, and presence—we got

that last one from *Star Search*—and that day she failed them all."
Celia gazed past Jeremy out the window. "I thought we should
make her go into the woods and Djuna thought that we should
give her a haircut, so instead of fight about it we decided to do
both."

When she closed her eyes she could picture the classroom
art cabinet and an institutional soup can containing scissors by
the blunt-tipped dozen, each waiting, blade-end down.

"It was the first time Leanne said no," Celia said. "She said
if we wanted to leave her out in the woods that was fine, but
no haircut. I could tell it wasn't going to happen that way
because of how quickly Djuna agreed. All of us met behind the
school that afternoon when the buses came. I knew Djuna had
the scissors. The first thing she did was tie Leanne's hands.
Leanne said, 'Please,' and I told Djuna that I didn't think it was
a good idea, but Djuna wouldn't listen. Leanne struggled at first
but then Josie helped me hold her, and I think she must have
decided it wasn't worth it. Djuna cut off all the hair in the back,
right above the neck, and then started in on the sides. I don't
know whether Leanne started to squirm, or if Djuna was just
being careless, but Leanne yelped and when Djuna pulled away
there was this little cut on Leanne's ear. It was small, the sort
of thing that happens with home haircuts sometimes, but
it scared even Djuna because she stopped right away and said
that the haircut was over and that we should head for the
woods. I told her I thought we'd done enough. I told her all
the way down Ripley Road, and around the curve. I mean,
we'd said that we hated each other plenty of times before, but
on that day . . ."

The silence at the dining room table was a glass bead the house held in its mouth.

"When I got on the bus that afternoon and you weren't there," Jeremy said, "I spent the whole ride wondering whether or not to tell. When Mom saw me, she decided that you'd gone to Djuna's, so I didn't bother to correct her. I figured that you'd owe me. Then the police brought you home." He shook his head. "I hid on the stairs. I thought Mom would make me go back to my room, but she never did. The first thing you did was throw up, right in the middle of the floor. You weren't crying or anything. Instead you had this look on your face like . . . I don't know, Cee. Like a part of you had been torn out."

"You saw the whole thing?"

He nodded. "Part of me wanted to go back to my room, or at least plug my ears, but I couldn't. And the more I listened, the more mad I got."

"At me?"

"At Djuna!" he said. "Seeing you like that . . . I mean, even *I* knew you weren't supposed to get into a stranger's car, and I was only eight!"

She examined her brother's face. "Jem," she began.

"I know," he said. "Mom told me what you say you remember. About the woods. I'm not going to try to contradict you, Cee, but it sure sounded to me that day like you were telling the truth."

She glanced away.

"Look," he said. "If it's at all helpful, my own memory's only perfect up to a certain point. Big sections of my high school years, the beginning of my recovery . . . they're just gone. When I was first getting myself together, I'd go some-place like the Quik Mart and someone would come up to me and be all like 'Hey man,' and I'd have no idea who they were."

"What would you do?"

"At first, I just stared through whoever it was like he was some kind of ghost, but that didn't seem right. I mean, it wasn't their fault that they remembered something I didn't. So even-tually I just started saying 'Hey' back and made small talk, say where I was at. It didn't cost me anything and it was over soon enough. And then I would get on with my life."

"I wasn't here," she said. "You were going through all this and I just . . . I should have stayed."

Jeremy smiled.

"Nope," he said. "You were where you were supposed to be. Off in Chicago, starting the next chapter of your life. To be honest, it probably would have been harder having you around instead of as this long-distance reminder of all the ways I was messing up. It's the curse of the little brother, living in someone's shadow. I was always doomed to be jealous, even about all that stuff with Djuna."

Celia's eyes widened.

"I know," he laughed. "It sounds crazy, but think of it this way: everyone started being extra nice to you! Like, we'd go to the library and the librarian would give you a book from the donations pile, or we'd go to the grocery store and the cashier would give you a piece of candy, not like you were even aware of it at the time. You were like a zombie, which is the only reason it worked. If you'd been like a normal kid, people would have stopped doing that stuff, which is how I realized I didn't want to be like you after all. You were way too sad."

Light from the window played across his face, casting the same old shadows.

"Do you ever worry?" Celia said. "Now that it's not just you? I'm not even talking about Daniel. Let's start with the idea of just being with another person. I think that all these years, part of me has been afraid that if I wasn't careful, I'd just . . . I mean, once you know what you're capable of, how can you be sure . . ."

"You can't," Jeremy said. "At first I was going to meetings about three times a day, and it still didn't feel like enough. But Daniel gives me something to focus on, plus just his being here reminds me of how different things are now."

"But don't you worry that one day—"

"All the time," he said. "I mean, I wake up every morning thinking about *exactly* what it would take to fuck it all up. But knowing how to do something isn't the same as doing it. So, I just decide over and over again not to. And, sure, it's way more work for me than other people, but I like to think that it's something everybody has to do. I'm doing it right now. And in one way or another, I bet that you are too."

Noreen poked her head through the doorway.

"Sorry to interrupt," she said, "but Pam says that Daniel's binky is in the car and you have the keys?"

"Is it naptime already?" Celia's brother headed for the door, gripping his keys as if they might bolt from his hands.

CHAPTER 23

Mrs. Pearson lived off a county road that had a name but was mostly known by its number, a two-lane highway dotted with fields, the occasional produce stand, and family homes whose yards bordered the road, inducing fear for the safety of their children. In the fading light, Celia didn't realize she had missed the turnoff until she reached the next town, the directions printed off the Web not having included a description of something narrow and unpaved, and marked only by the dilapidated stone foundation of the small house just preceding it.

The road seemed less a road than an encroachment into the woods. At irregular intervals, mailboxes with peeling numbers on their sides marked gravel driveways. Celia suspected that people who lived here year-round made a proud habit of being snowed in. Thick foliage allowed for occasional glimpses of houses. Most were clad in exuberantly rustic wood shingles spared from silliness only by the dignity of the surrounding trees. The house at the end of Mrs. Pearson's drive was older and simpler than the rest. Celia could imagine a woodsman building it for his family, back when people made their own clothes and children walked miles to school in all weather. This might have made it charming if Celia hadn't felt as if she were the last living person on earth. In town, the bark of a dog or the grumble of a passing car resembled urban silence enough to put her at ease, but here even the wind chime dangling from the awning was still. Celia tried and failed to imagine Djuna's mother inside.

The front door opened just as she reached to knock.

"I'm sorry!" Mrs. Pearson said. "Did I startle you?"

Celia was blindsided by the smell of cinnamon. "I'm fine, I was just—" She closed her eyes and found herself in Djuna's foyer: there was the antique writing desk covered with the day's mail; to the left, the staircase with its burgundy runner; to the right, the dark wood-framed mirror on a wall the color of a cloudless sky. Opened eyes brought dislocation. Only the scent remained.

"Oh my goodness, it really is you," said Mrs. Pearson. "When I got off the phone I wasn't sure. I thought maybe I'd been daydreaming. You see, in the back of my mind I always thought that as long as I stayed listed, one day you might . . ." She smiled. She was wearing a blouse Celia thought she remembered, an ivory-colored silk with pearl buttons and tapered sleeves that showed off her hands. Mrs. Pearson's face had aged, and the dark hair that wound into the familiar bun was filigreed with gray, but she was Djuna's mother still. "Celia, you look exactly like I thought you would. You look wonderful. Would you mind if I . . . How silly. I don't need to ask permission! Come here so I can give you a hug!"

Mrs. Pearson's hugs were the whole-body immersions Celia's family reserved for very bad news. Even as a child, Celia knew better than to resist. Before, she had been enclosed at belly level. Today Mrs. Pearson's mouth aligned with her shoulder.

"Look at you," Djuna's mother whispered.

She held Celia at arm's length and stared, her gaze starting at Celia's head and working its way down. Twenty-one years ago, Celia hadn't noticed the resemblance between mother and daughter, but they shared the same protuberant eyes, the same sharp chin.

"Welcome to my home," Mrs. Pearson said.

A small living room opened onto an equally small kitchen, a table visible through the doorway. To the right, a hall led to what could only be the bedroom. There was no familiar furniture. In place of the pomegranate couch, the living room contained a small beige love seat and matching recliner. In lieu of photographs, colored glass bottles lined the ledge of the room's picture window.

"I knew that you would have become a young woman," Mrs. Pearson continued, "that of course you would have grown up . . . but we should sit down. Do you remember those cookies, the ones with the cinnamon on top?"

"Snickerdoodles," Celia said, the name leaping the twenty-one-year void.

"Every time you came you would ask for them, so as soon as we got off the phone I made up a batch. You're not one of those people always on some diet, are you? You certainly don't need to be; you've turned into a lovely thing—but I'm babbling. You can't imagine how uninterested I am in hearing my own voice. I want to hear all about you."

She led Celia through the kitchen doorway to a small square table whose constituent parts Celia could picture arriving for assembly with a wordless schematic, a bag of bolts, and an Allen wrench. The sight of cookies arranged on a ceramic plate with a familiar green stripe conjured the old octagonal table of reddish wood, the hard-backed chairs with their cheerily mismatched seat cushions, kitchen walls the color of lemon sorbet, and a white floor on which Djuna and Celia would skate in their socks, pretending to be in the Ice Capades.

"I used to have more things," Mrs. Pearson murmured, running her finger along the plate's painted edge, "but it wasn't good for me. My doctor told me to get rid of them, and I mostly listened. Mostly." She smiled. "I still have photos, of course. I only take them out on her birthday, but if you'd like we can look through them together. Do you want coffee or tea? The coffee is already brewed and the kettle is on the boil, so neither is any trouble."

Had Celia asked for honeysuckle nectar, Mrs. Pearson would have run to gather blooms.

"Coffee is fine, thank you."

There was a tray already set with teacups, milk, and sugar. The kitchen was too small to hold more than one cook. As Djuna's mother poured, Celia abandoned her initial vision of an imaginary woodsman and his children.

"So, you've fled west," Mrs. Pearson said. "How long have you been in Chicago?"

"I went for college and never left."

"Chicago." She chuckled. "Dennis would have loved for us to live there. He was heartbroken when Northwestern and the University of Chicago turned him down, but I thought Jensenville was a much better place to raise a child." She shook her head. "So much safer, you know." She reached for a cookie and made a dunking motion into a cup that wasn't there before reaching for the one left on the tray. "And then when the university also offered me a position in the English department, well, it was hardly an offer we could refuse. Do you know that if Djuna had been a boy, Dennis would have insisted on naming her Malthus? What kind of name is that? There are no good nicknames! Whereas Djuna allows for June, or Una. When she was very little, I called her Jujube, but she put the kibosh on that by the time she was six."

"I've never met anyone else with that name," Celia said.

"I'm not surprised," Mrs. Pearson said. "Do you know of Djuna Barnes?"

"Wasn't she an author?"

"And a lesbian," Mrs. Pearson added. "Now if she had been a heterosexual . . ." She shook her head. "As if lesbianism is contagious! But it's a beautiful name, and she was a beautiful writer. Of course, had Dennis known, he wouldn't have liked it one bit. Dennis fancied himself more open-minded than your average mathematician. I suppose he was, but that's not saying much, is it? He's in Michigan now. You don't remember him, do you?"

"I can picture his face," Celia said. "I remember the dolls he brought back from his trips."

Once, she and Djuna had undressed the most beautiful one—a Japanese girl with perfect black hair and a fancy kimono. They used cuticle scissors to undo the stitches, the layers of cloth coming away in pieces, the kimono reduced to scraps of cheap silk.

Mrs. Pearson smirked. "Of course you do. I remember the look on your face whenever Djuna showed them as proof. Of having a father, that is, and not just a tenant in the upstairs bedroom office." She laughed. "I fell in love with his mind, you know, which for a while gave us something in common. Do you know that he actually kept a framed copy of his Wechsler scores? I was certain a woman of letters and a man of mathematical genius could make a child of boundless potential. Which I suppose in a way turned out to be true."

Djuna's mother stared at the wall. Celia realized a beauty mark she had always taken for natural was something Mrs. Pearson penciled onto the skin.

The silence stretched. Celia was accustomed to their conversation as a dance in which she was led through the turns.

"How are your parents?" Mrs. Pearson asked.

"Good!" Celia chorused, her smile too broad, her mind leaping in five directions. "They're beginning to talk about

retiring, but I don't think they'd know what to do with themselves . . . Um, Mrs. Pearson? I'm sorry my mother didn't keep
in touch."

"Celia." Djuna's mother sighed. "You're thirty-two years
old. I think you can call me Grace, don't you?" She encircled
her cup with tapered, elegant fingers. "And please don't feel
the need to apologize for your mother. We weren't particular
friends. It was always such a nice idea, an adult friendship flowering from one between children, but what were you supposed
to talk about after you'd exhausted the topics of their teachers
and their little triumphs and foibles? I found it so . . . depress-
ing to predicate friendship on the sole shared criteria of both
being mammals who'd borne live young."

When Djuna's mother smiled, her face softened. "Of
course I don't blame your mother. I really don't. In the end,
she only did what everyone else did, which I'm sure is what I
would have done had the situation been reversed. I mean, what
can one say or do under the circumstance? You can never talk
about the thing you're both thinking of, which is that one of
you still has a child."

Mrs. Pearson had once made Celia dream of brightly
painted houses, each containing a mother who spoke fast and
knowing. *Sophisticated* was the word she had struck upon in
fifth grade and repeated as a silent accompaniment to terms and
topics beyond her comprehension. Sometimes after she and
Djuna had fought, she and Mrs. Pearson would spend whole
afternoons together while Djuna sulked in her room.

Djuna's mother bit into another cookie, then placed it
beside the one she had already taken. "I suppose that's the point

of belonging to a church," she continued. "So that there's always someone to stick by you. Which is why we atheists are all so attached to our shrinks." She laughed abruptly, a sound like the bark of a seal. "An expensive proposition, atheism. A chaplain would have been much more economical."

Celia had forgotten the old fear, the temporary sense of audience, the certainty that she was on the verge of being dismissed.

"Tell me," Mrs. Pearson continued. "How has your poetry come along? You wrote such lovely poems, quite exceptional for your age."

The conversation was turning into an exam for which Celia had studied all the wrong subjects.

"I haven't written for a while," she said. "I kept it up through college, but not really after."

Djuna's mother looked at her, then looked somewhere else.

"I had hopes for you, dear," she admitted. "Back then you had sparkle. At the time I thought it was the sparkle of a poet, but perhaps it was just youth. Whatever it was, it rubbed off on Djuna. She certainly didn't get it from me or Dennis. We were never popular children. So you can just imagine what it was like coming here and seeing her blossom. She'd always had such trouble making friends."

Celia pictured Djuna's dark braids, her pale neck. That first day in class, Djuna hadn't once turned in her chair. She'd sat perfectly still, save for when she raised her hand, her entire being committed to being called by name.

"I always thought it was something about her that rubbed off on me," Celia said.

Mrs. Pearson smiled. "Then the two of you must have brought out the best in each other."

"Oh, I don't know about that." Celia's mouth had gone dry. She swallowed her coffee, which Djuna's mother reached to refill before she had released the cup. "I remember us fighting a lot."

"Of course you did!" Mrs. Pearson said. "You were girls! And you were so competitive. I remember once I came into Djuna's room to find you two simply screaming at each other over a game of Monopoly. Djuna had landed on a utility, and you said you wouldn't let her buy it until she pronounced the words on the card correctly. Djuna was certain it was pronounced 'tittle deed,' but you weren't having any of that. So you consulted the resident English professor and then you insisted that Djuna apologize."

"That's not how I remember it," Celia told her.

"Of course it isn't," Mrs. Pearson said. "That's what mothers are for."

The clock on the wall filled the room with its ticking. Celia imagined hours magnified by the sound.

"Grace?" she asked. "What do you remember about that day?"

"Is that what we're going to talk about now?" she asked softly.

"I'd like to," Celia said.

Djuna's mother gazed at her lap. Her hands grasped at each other, palm pressed against palm. "Shall I tell you what she ate for breakfast?" she began. "Blueberry yogurt and orange juice. I wanted her to have a bran muffin, but she wouldn't, so instead

I stuck one in her backpack for later on. Shall I tell you what she was wearing?"

"Her purple pants with the extra pockets," Celia answered. "Her white Tretorns with the pink laces. Her light blue unicorn shirt, and her light blue jacket. She hated when you put muffins in her backpack. She gave them to Ed."

"Who was Ed?" Mrs. Pearson whispered.

"The boy who sat behind us on the bus. He did whatever we told him to do."

Djuna's mother smiled. "Of course he did."

"We weren't very nice to him."

"You didn't have to be," Mrs. Pearson said. "You didn't have to be nice to anyone. You were such confident girls. I loved that about you, that confidence. Up until the last day, I had no idea there was such a thing as too much."

She tilted her head to one side, as if to observe Celia from a different angle. Celia held her breath.

"She began as such a sensible girl," Mrs. Pearson continued. "Do you know that she never once went into the street by herself when she was little? Not once. I told her, 'Djuna, that's where the cars go. It's not safe unless you're holding a grown-up's hand,' and that was all it took. It was so nice not to have to worry about her in that way. Were you like that as a little girl? Sensible?"

Celia told her that she didn't know.

"I'm sure you were," Mrs. Pearson said. "Your mother was a sensible woman. She certainly didn't approve of me. She wanted to, of course, but I think I was too much for her. Anyway, I'm sure you listened when she advised you to stay out of the street, and not to talk to strangers, and certainly never to get into a stranger's car."

Mrs. Pearson closed her eyes, then opened them again. "Your mother never raised her voice. Not with you or anyone else. It was a fundamental difference between us and one I don't think she could get over."

Djuna's mother placed one hand against her cheek in mock surprise. "When I get upset, you see—as you well know—I yell. And I defy anyone who says that it's not a solution. It is. I almost always feel better afterward. Of course, when you came to my door that day, you weren't yelling. You were so upset that you could hardly speak. I asked you questions, but you were crying so hard and the other girls were no help, they were crying too, and you were all just saying the same thing over and over. Then the police arrived and took you away with them, and I never saw you again."

Mrs. Pearson looked at Celia in astonishment. "I never saw you again!" Her cup shook as she raised it to her mouth. "You were never mine, but I missed you all the same." She replaced the cup and hid her trembling hand. "Of course, it helped to know that you were somewhere out in the world. It became a consolation. Though I had always imagined you becoming a poet. Not someone who goes through a poetic phase, mind you, but an actual poet."

Celia smiled. "Sorry to disappoint you."

"Never apologize for what you are, dear. But tell me, seeing as you're not a poet, what *do* you do?"

"I'm a performance auditor for the Illinois Auditor General," she said.

Mrs. Pearson's face went slack. "I have absolutely no idea what that is."

"It means," Celia said, "that I examine state agencies—Child Protective Services, the Department of Juvenile Corrections, the Department of Health, the Department of Environmental Quality—to report on how well their programs are meeting their goals. Then the State Assembly drafts proposals to help those programs run better. Through increased funding, for example, or improved legislation."

"That sounds terribly useful," Grace drawled.

"It is!" Celia said. She had planned which stories to tell and in what order, but Djuna's mother was staring past her.

"And are you married?" Mrs. Pearson asked.

"I live with a public high school history teacher named Huck," Celia said. "We own an apartment near Logan Square and we've got two dogs named Bella and Sylvie, and—"

"Two *dogs*, how precious," Mrs. Pearson said. "How charming. But surely you and Huck must be trying for the *richest* experience life can offer?"

Because Celia was taller now, Mrs. Pearson looked different than she had when Celia was a girl, her face flatter than the one Celia had to crane her neck to see.

"No," Celia said. "Not yet."

"How very modern of you," Mrs. Pearson cooed. "It must be wonderful to be so young and modern."

"Mrs. Pearson," Celia said. "Are you all right? You seem a little upset."

"Upset?" Djuna's mother smiled. "Why, I'm just *ducky*!

You can't imagine how excited I was to hear your voice on the phone. My own Celia! Returned to me after twenty-one years! I was so greatly looking forward to our conversation. Back then, I had told myself that you were like a beautiful empty pitcher that I was filling up with sparkling water." She leaned across the table. Celia had never seen her eyes so close, their gray-green irises ringed at the center by a circle of brownish-gold.

"I used to comfort myself with the thought that you had survived," Grace whispered. "That you had gone on to become something extraordinary."

Her face had become strange, as if it were a hand liable to grab whatever came within reach. It was an expression of terrifying possibility, which Celia now realized she had sighted twenty-one years before at the edge of a road, on a girl with the same sharp chin, in the last moment that their brief friendship had known.

Mrs. Pearson sat very still, and Celia found herself counting the same way she used to after a lightning flash, in order to gauge the distance of the storm.

Djuna's mother blinked several times. Her mouth twisted into something that was nearly a smile. "I'm so glad you came, Celia, but I don't want to keep you any longer. I'm sure your mother has made all sorts of plans. Please, take the cookies. I made them especially for you." She blew a short puff of air at Celia, then leaned back as if having extinguished a candle.

"Oh," Celia said, rising from her chair. "Thank you, Mrs. . . . Thank you, Grace."

"You're very welcome. And do take care backing out of the drive. It's not a terribly busy road, but another car on it can be so damn hard to see."

Celia crossed the living room as quickly as she could. The outside quiet felt reassuring now and she inhaled it in slow, deep breaths. The darkening sky above the tree line was electric blue. Celia was not immediately able to fit her key into the car's ignition but once she had steadied her hand, the engine turned. She backed out carefully, just as Mrs. Pearson had instructed, and slowly made her way to the county road.

Celia rolled down the windows and let the air pound around her, the sound of it filling her ears. Her bag was almost packed, her ticket waiting. By this time tomorrow, she and Huck would be home.

That afternoon, it was warm and her shirt clung to her back. Her face had yet to be shaped by an individual nose; her skin was still unlined velvet; her shoes waited to be outgrown. She was out of breath from running, and her heart hammered inside her chest. She thought of all that she was ready to say to Djuna, and how if that didn't end things between them, they could hunt four-leafed clovers on the rest of the walk home. Celia rounded the curve, and Djuna's anger wafted back to her from the road's edge in waves of sour air tinged with exhaust. The brown car was not Mrs. Pearson's Volvo, or any other car that Celia knew. When Djuna turned, her face was equally unfamiliar. It was a face of terrifying possibility, ready to pull, or to be pulled in. It was a face capable of anything.

ACKNOWLEDGMENTS

Thanks to Nathan Englander, David Gassaway, Ellen and Mark Goldberg, Saryn Goldberg, Tim Kreider, Adrienne and Michael Little, Lisa Rosenthal, Anthony Tognazzini, Ellen Twaddell, and Michael Wilde. Thanks to Wendy Schmalz and Bill Thomas. Thanks to Hannah Miriam Belinfante, cataloger for the NYPL Dorot Jewish Division, for her research assistance; and to Melanie Chesney, Performance Auditor Director for the state of Arizona, for so generously sharing her time and knowledge. Thank you, Jason, from beginning to end.